D0409763

The Seven Deadly Sins

A Celebration of Virtue and Vice

Edited by Rosalind Porter

Preface by Alex Clark

Union
Books

DUN LAOGHAIRE-
RATHDOWN LIBRARIES

DLR20001010114

BERTRAMS	19/11/2012
	£12.99
EA	

Individual contributions copyright by the authors.
Copyright © Nicola Barker 2012; © Dylan Evans 2012;
© David Flusfeder 2012; © Todd McEwen 2012; © Martin Rowson 2012;
© Ali Smith 2012; © John Sutherland 2012.

The quotation from *Harvey* by Mary Chase is used by permission of
Josef Weinberger Plays Ltd.

The moral right of the contributors to be identified as the authors of this
work has been asserted by them in accordance with the Copyright,
Designs and Patents Act 1988.

All rights reserved. No part of this book may be reproduced or utilised in any
form or by any means, electronic or mechanical, including photocopying,
recording or by any information storage and retrieval system,
without permission in writing from Union Books.

A catalogue record for this book is available from the British Library.

ISBN 978-1-90-852615-1

1 3 5 7 9 10 8 6 4 2

2012 2014 2016 2015 2013

Typeset by SX Composing DTP, Rayleigh, Essex

Printed and bound in Great Britain by
MPG Books, Bodmin, Cornwall

'Two things awe me most, the starry sky above me and the moral law within me.' Immanuel Kant

'The more successful the villain, the more successful the picture.' Alfred Hitchcock

SINS

PREFACE

Has sin disappeared? Certainly the furious God described in John Sutherland's survey of wrath, who could barely let a day go by without seeking retribution for humanity's misdemeanours, has retreated from view, presumably deafened by our collective complaint: *O Lord, you're really stepping on my buzz.* We're a little easier on ourselves these days; should someone, perhaps in the process of *opening up* to you, confide that they're feeling a bit guilty about something they've done, or not done, or said, or not said, then your reply might default to a variation of: 'Come on: don't beat yourself up about it.' In fact, if you didn't, you'd run the risk of being accused of being unsupportive, itself a tributary of one of the modern sins.

Clearly, it's not the case that transgressive behaviour

has ceased to exist; more that we've found ways to deal with it that don't catapult us so swiftly into the crime-and-punishment grid of Judeo-Christian theology. Sometimes it's repackaged and relabelled; frequently dissected so that we might examine its genesis and its complex evolution; occasionally subjected to vigorous reclassification so that it finally emerges as not sinful at all. Historical context, social conditioning, cultural differences, psychiatry and psychology – all make their appearance in our quest to establish, for once and for all, to anyone who might be listening, that, really, truly, we haven't done a thing wrong.

Is this so – dare I use the word? – 'bad'? Not many of us, surely, would stampede to the polls to vote for a return to the dreadful old days when schoolboys lived in fear of blindness, helping yourself to an extra chocolate after dinner required full-scale weeping and gnashing of teeth and you could buy flails and scourges by the dozen. And that's before you even get on to the really serious Ten Commandments stuff, such as coveting thy neighbour's wife (now helpfully rebranded as 'swinging'; not sure how the oxen and the ass fit in).

Perhaps not. But downgrading the very idea of deadly sin – the seven have, after all, lasted in one form or another for an impressively long time – brings its own problems. Not least: amateurism. In the absence of a wrathful deity, everyone's an expert. Each day and each night, our online communities swarm with witchfinder generals on the hunt for imperfect behaviour, travelling alone but sometimes joining forces to shine a light on those they deem miscreants. They have proved that judgementalism is perhaps the most powerful rocket fuel available to us, although it appears to react badly when mixed with an unexpected apology or the production of contrary evidence or, most damagingly of all, a more potent brand of righteousness.

What does this tell us? It has, rarely, to do with genuinely vicious or aberrant behaviour, in the face of which we still tend to defer to traditional, institutional authority; it appears to cohere far more readily to trivial offences, or to questions of taste and propriety. Is it, then, simply a reflection of our uneasy feeling that someone, somewhere needs to be in the wrong to keep the morality seesaw perfectly balanced? Or an expression of our fear that a life without sin and the consequent chastisements is a life dizzyingly free of boundaries?

The writers in this anthology demonstrate that, in the modern world, sin is a complex business; indeed, a preliminary defining of terms is often very much in order. David Flusfeder, for example, argues in his memoir of a complicated romantic entanglement that 'lust is sexual desire with a bad press agent' (he also demonstrates that taking the object of your affection to watch drugged sharks swim around a cramped tank isn't the best guarantee of success). And Todd McEwen, despite his pronouncement that 'we're all in hell anyway and already', is at pains to point out that sloth is quite different from straightforward laziness; a slothful person can be terribly busy (even if they'd probably prefer not to be). We hope that he recovers from his endeavours soon, although we're not optimistic given his admission that after any great mental or physical effort 'I tend to pant, for two or three years, before attempting anything further'.

For Dylan Evans, who defends greed against its many detractors, that effort might be a defining human characteristic; his piece speaks up for those who prefer life on the treadmill than life in a hammock. 'Some people want more than others,' he writes. 'Is this a defect in those who want more, or in those who want less?' A tricky question to answer, though wanting less would have done both of the two prodigious eaters in Martin Rowson's graphic depiction of gluttony a bit of good. Not a piece for anyone with a weak stomach.

It is often the case that fiction can sneak up on a subject and take it by surprise; and so it proves in both Ali Smith's story 'The Modern Psyche' and Nicola Barker's 'Young Versus Old'. Smith's exploration of envy spirals out of a ribbon of discarded orange peel, taking in Ovid and Melanie Klein on the way, and producing a splendid inversion. Envy, as one of the characters in her two-hander confidently declaims, is not about wanting what belongs to someone else; 'mostly it's about wanting the other person not to have what he or she's got'. And in Barker's clear-eyed – if typographically exuberant – look at that most contemporary of sins, vanity, what people want – and probably want others not to have – is youth and eternal life. But do they know what they're asking for?

This book is not one to be read in the spirit of Puritanism; it will respond far more happily to the silk kimono than the hair shirt. That is not to say that we do not encourage rigour and thoughtfulness. The more elusive sin seems to be, the more difficult to define and the more minutely anatomised, the more fascinating it is. But reading does not itself seem to have been outlawed, so indulge yourself. As the good book has it, 'let us eat and drink, for tomorrow we die'.

Alex Clark
October 2012

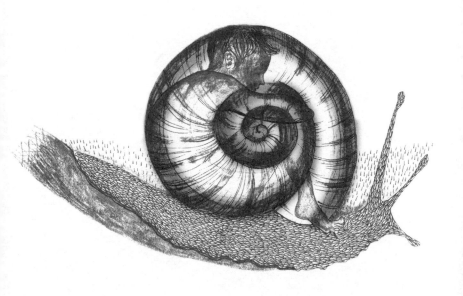

Sloth

Todd McEwen

CHUMLEY: I know where I'd go. I'd go to Pittsburgh. There's a roadhouse outside Pittsburgh, in a grove of maple trees. Cool – green – beautiful. I'd go there with a beautiful young woman. A strange woman. A quiet woman. I wouldn't even want to know her name. I would send out for some cold beer. I'd tell her things – things that I've never told anyone. Things that are locked in here. *(Beats his breast.)* I'd want her to stretch out a soft, cool hand and stroke my head and say, 'Poor thing! Oh, you poor, poor thing!'

ELWOOD: How long would you want this to go on?

CHUMLEY: Three weeks.

ELWOOD: Cold beer, Pittsburgh and 'Poor, poor thing' for three weeks? Wouldn't that get a trifle monotonous?

CHUMLEY: No, no, it would not. It would be wonderful!

Mary Chase, *Harvey*

Is it really a sin, dear friend, sitting here, looking at the river? The qualities of water in summer. A 'sin'? I don't think so. An *investigation*. And we're all in hell anyway and already. Aren't you in hell? Yes you are. So the idea that these things, these 'sins' can get us *damned*, rather than tickled, or reprimanded at the most, is pretty silly. Worse than silly – disingenuous. 'Sin'!

But in contemplating sloth I've become terrified. Have I got it? Did I already have it, or have I acquired it through contemplating it?

HIGHWAYS AND BYWAYS OF SLOTH

Bosch painted some panels illustrative of the 'Seven Deadly Sins'. They don't look like he cared much; of course he had horrors more important than manufactured ones to concern himself with. Busy guy. In his treatment of sloth, a perfectly decent-looking older fellow is asleep in an armchair. His dog is asleep on the floor beside him. I mean, excuse me but he *had a duty to his dog* to provide her some warmth and comfort!

Some are born to sloth and some have sloth thrust upon them. In my own case I had parents who were descendants of the Work Ethic, but they'd been a little derailed by the Depression and World War II. They functioned, but we knew that they didn't quite see the point. They were on the verge of stasis, which was lucky for us.

But then came television: KNXT, KNBC, KTLA, KABC, KHJ, KTTV and KCOP. Quite a lot of television to start off the 1950s with. You crazy little Brits. Most important were KNXT (*Captain Kangaroo*), KHJ (*Engineer Bill*), KTTV (*Sheriff John's Lunch Brigade*) and KCOP (*Felix the Cat*). We developed the sole habit and preoccupation of *looking*, and not in a particularly healthy way. Looking and not doing. Sloth?

Later came UHF stations from Mexico City that broadcast only *telenovelas* and the *corrida*. We found a slothful way of torturing our cousin, whom we hated, with the *telenovelas*: we would pretend that we understood what was being said. Watching the *corrida* seemed corrupt even to me, even though I had no morals to speak of. To lie there and watch a live animal, a big animal, killed with big picks and swords while you suck down grape pop. It didn't feel right, but I had no idea where I'd got the idea that it didn't feel right.

My cat liked the *corrida*!

I was dimly aware of my father's exasperation with us on Saturday mornings. Like many parents in 1959 he was annoyed and terrified that we watched kiddie shows from five in the morning till noon solid. I was aware of this *general* exasperation, too – in fact cartoons themselves made fun of grouchy, carping parents. I somehow convinced myself that it wasn't really me they were worried about, even though I could feel awfully ill around 10 a.m. after three giant bowls of sugary cereal, squinting at the television in a room with no natural light or ventilation. When you live in your pyjamas, to emerge finally into the torpid day, your father flinging the curtains open and voicing not only despair but genuine *woe*, trying to shock you out of inactivity, this could make you feel pretty crumby. He never used the word *sloth* because he hated the Bible. But he was muttering something.

At school I observed and did not participate. Sometimes I became so sleepy, and so bored, that I would raise my hand, as if asking to go to the toilet, get up without taking my coat or any of my things and walk home, enter the house without announcing my presence, lie down on my bed and wait for my mother to discover me. Does this count as sloth, or as rebellion? Or both? The Revolt of the Slothful.

I wanted my own place to pee. I could understand nothing about plumbing; it seemed so organic and mysterious. So I prudently and simply obtained a large ice-cream carton and put it in my closet. When in the middle of a complicated Erector Set project I next needed to pee, I stepped into the closet as if it were my brand new personal bathroom and urinated into the carton. *Voilà*, problem solved. A sense of demesne achieved. The eventual discovery of my methods, which were nothing really but a pursuit of *richesse*, I leave to your imagination. Was this sloth, or stupidity? And if the latter, why is that not a 'sin'?

What is Doddling ?

School itself is sloth, if sloth is, as God has suggested through his executive suite, not living up to your potential. School exists to kill *all* potential. In 1962 I was told I could not take my arithmetic test with my favourite pencil. The pencil that had loved and stood by me. It was well over two inches in diameter and had a squat Chinese man of wood on the end instead of an eraser. I could barely lift it. But it was the only pencil I could conceive of taking the test with and I failed, *failed*.

Every day when I went off to school, my mother said, 'Don't doddle on the way home'. I didn't know what doddling was, though in moral sloth I promised not to. When I finally found out it was *dawdling* (I think I asked the ice-cream man) I was filled with resentment that they thought me capable of it. I was a nervous kid and I really shot home every day to the safety of our arid house and television and my cat, who was rather good at relaxing and so was a comfort to me (are cats thought to be slothful?).

Is worry sloth? I suspect that it is.

I began to fear that I might be dawdling without knowing it. How – would you cross your legs? Walk backward, or in a circle from time to time? Then I got the idea that dawdling had to do with hedges, doing something under a hedge, not that there were any – it just sounded like that. I had seen period children in movies and engravings banging sticks on fences, playing with *hoops*. Now *that's* dawdling. But is it sloth?

Would the friend I walked purposefully home with every day suddenly see or sense that I was dawdling and betray me? And if so, some friend!

Perhaps all modern childhood is sloth; all this newly minted time out. We were watchers, at war with work. Which boiled around us. At the age of nine I somehow managed to drag my father into a place where older boys paid to race tiny electric cars. There was nothing remotely attractive about the model cars, the people or the place, even to me. Yet I felt this could become an *interest*. The guys all in dirty white T-shirts.

Was this more slothful than watching TV? Yes.

These tiny cars *symbolised cars*, which were eventually to become our undoing, environmentally and economically. This was sort of brilliant – you spent all your dough on these little cars and watched them go round and around. Just like when you grew up.

Jesus Christ, said my father, who pays for this? I

have to get out of Los Angeles. (Notice that he said *he* had to get out.)

The weird thing was that some of these dirty T-shirt guys were old enough to have cars, actual cars. But they were sticking with these. The sloth cars.

Sloth is not purely laziness; some very busy people are slothful. Because they don't think. But is sloth a *kind* of leisure? Take the Case of the van der Wijk Bathrobes. My school friend Andre van der Wijk invited me to spend a Friday night at his house. We would watch Ray Harryhausen's *Jason and the Argonauts*, eat popcorn, and in the dark exchange the usual confidences of eleven-year-olds. OK. So I got there and realised Andre's entire family were going to watch *Jason and the Argonauts*; what is more, each had a plush or even *fulsome* bathrobe – *family TV-viewing bathrobes*. It looked like a magazine ad for TV sets. I had only my thin summer pyjamas. Andre's father insisted I be given an Argonaut-viewing robe. The point was that they weren't lounging, weren't being slothful. The viewing robes meant that a serious family event was taking place. If I'd watched the movie at home I'd have been upside down half the time, my feet on the wall and my pyjamas stuck to my butt.

This led to an interest in the *pyjamas of other lands*, particularly nightshirts, which I had never seen but associated with somnolence if not sloth: there was a chain of motels whose trademark was a bear in nightshirt and cap, his eyes half-closed and his front legs extended as if he were sleepwalking. His name was *Sleepy*.

There was a character that often appeared on a kiddie show, also in a nightshirt, carrying a large candlestick. He would suddenly walk through a scene in progress, stopping everyone, heave a tremendous yawn, and head upstairs. His name was *Mr Attic*. I have since looked for him almost every day of my existence.

Stan Laurel's choice of winter wear, a nightshirt, long johns and enormous socks, is now my own, since I live in a cold place. But Stan Laurel had energy.

In middle school I was slothful. I had too many hormones, or not enough, I can't remember. Anyway it's pretty common. I felt and looked like a slug. But this was the only period in my life when I ever actually punched anyone in the face, so you be the judge.

When I was fifteen, my father suggested to me that I might want to get married. 'For sexual satisfaction'. Because I was drowning in sperm and bankrupting the family with Kleenex. But to me this seemed a slothful solution. After all, hadn't I an education ahead of me? And who would support my new household? Surely that would cost more than all the Kleenex in Christendom. And, above all else, I thought, *who will choose my bride?*

The Perception Of Sloth

Whenever I've got anywhere, physically or mentally, it's taken a lot of effort, so I tend to pant, for two or three years, before attempting anything further. Is this recuperation? Calculation? Calibration? *Sloth?* Such an effort was going from school to university.

There I had a very clever girlfriend, who knew almost everything about me from the moment we met. So *that* wasn't going to work out.

We were at the zoo in the park. Past the monkeys and their painful and popular erections was a cage with a sloth in it (*Choloepus hoffmanni*). Once a day a keeper came by and with a long pole with a hook on the end he would gently lift the sloth out of its tree and put it on the ground (this used to amuse me because I thought it was like getting the 'hook' in vaudeville). They did this so that the hoi polloi could watch the sloth comically locomote.

This might have been unkind. A sloth gets along the ground awkwardly; it's reluctant to uncurl its paws, which aren't like hands or feet, but more like the top of a fireman's ladder. But perhaps even sloths get bored, and maybe a few minutes on the ground each day quickened its inner life. Maybe it thought, *This is really living.*

Was there something admirable in this little chap, I thought, or at least some slap in the face for the Bible? Everyone has some ambition, at least to eat. But sloths don't. To move from tree to tree, they wait for the wind to blow them close enough to the next so they can grab on.

Surely this is the apogee of calmness, if not out-and-out Buddhism.

They eat fruit only, fruit that is *handy*, one suspects, although I once met some people from Venezuela who were 'fruitarians', if that really is a word, and their existence was far from restful. Sloths are camouflaged by an alga that grows on them, which does seem a bit lazy. They are nocturnal, silent, inoffensive and solitary, normally producing only one offspring. Is *that* enough sex for the New Testament? Can the sloth's existence be said to be slothful? Isn't that judgement up to his fellows?

More importantly, could my girl see all these things when she looked in my eyes?

There he went, let's not say agonisingly, let's say *deliberately*, along the concrete walk of the zoo. The little animal. My girl watched him for a few minutes and then turned to me. She was wearing an expensive coat her father had given her. What she said she said kindly: 'You think that things happen *to* you.'

She'd realized I wasn't someone who was going to take charge, make things happen. This is what she said to me after a couple of minutes of watching the sloth get unhooked from its perch and meander nauseously about on the ground because it didn't have the right appurtenances. I mean after all, I was just trying to catch my *breath* after getting all the way to *New York*.

I tried to tell her that the little guy was an example to us all, that he was acting out the twentieth century, that he was the tortured hirsute character Beckett never wrote. But she hadn't read Beckett and she didn't care.

So that was pretty much it. And man was she right, that's what's so... Some days it is all I can do to get across the concrete. With my little hooks. But I am sure you feel the same.

Is Somnolence Sloth ?

I had a job where I had to think intensely but in very short bursts. This office was very warm. After several of these bursts my mind would wander. My colleague could sense my mind wandering, even though she typed with her back to me. When it started wandering she would stop typing and we would look out of the large plate-glass window together. 'How pleasant,' she would say, especially if it was raining out and we felt superior to all the wet people, with our lapsang souchong tea. Then she would start typing again. I once took this utterance as a proposal of marriage. That seems a little slothful.

The main bugger about these bursts and the wandering in the heating was that this was invariably when our employer's wife would enter the premises. She thought I was never working (untrue, so much for the power of seeing) and that I was lousy at arithmetic (true).

I was sometimes somnolent, rarely indolent. But my incompetence at invoicing made me slothful in her eyes; she saw sloth where there was none. Or not much. It *wasn't fair*. But a constant plaint for *fairness* is slothful, according to most members of the US Congress.

Is Ebriety Sloth ?

I have lived on my street for over a decade. When I go into the bar on the corner, the same two guys are always standing there, always in the exact same spot. One is short and dark with a baseball cap. The other, tall, has spectacles and no hair. They drink gallons of beer every day. They have remained completely unchanged in the entire ten years I have observed them. Is this sloth? It looks like hard work.

When you get down to it, why isn't drunkenness on the list? Forget *sloth*. Getting inked beyond belief seems a greater offence to the cosmic order than just sleeping in an armchair. Your dog curled up on the floor.

The only conclusion that can be drawn is that there was hardly any booze in the world when they wrote the Bible. So we ran rings around God.

Is Leisure Sloth ?

Yes. Because if you haven't noticed, 'leisure' is an outmoded concept. In the world of today you're either permanently unemployed or going nuts. Which will it be?

TONY BLAIR'S BIG BOOK OF NOTHING!

You have your *paragons of sloth*, if that is not a contradiction. Samuel Beckett's Murphy, certainly, and it's amusing that the great literary exemplar of sloth, Oblomov, was the nickname of Murphy's creator, given to him by his girlfriend Peggy Guggenheim. Who was a doer. In the 1930s, Beckett liked to stop in bed, as who does not.

You have Little Jack Horner, you have Albert the Alligator, you have George Bush senior, Humpty Dumpty, Jabba the Hutt. Maybe there's a character in the Bible who dithered or sat around. Who knows?

But *Tony Blair*. This man turned sloth from an un-thinking, confused, lowly error of unreconstructed bumpkins into high art, no, into *SIN*. Not only did he do nothing at all in his entire lifetime, but he stopped a lot of other people from doing or being able to do any-thing. *He digitised sloth and made it communicable.* It's quite a perversion, to make everything no longer real.

You start by making the internet the most important thing in everyone's life. You ruin the mails and make privacy sound like something people ought not to want. You turn people's health and the education of their children over to accountants.

It's not true that if you do nothing, nothing happens. Quite a lot happens. People get angry with you. You get thrown out of where you live. Look at Tony Blair – he did absolutely nothing at all, and tremendous amounts of shit came down. Just not on *him*. Of course *now* he is a Man of Affairs, and makes a pretty penny. But it all started with that really clever, really inspired, who knows, Christian-motivated doing of *bupkis*.

The newspapers said recently that Tony Blair is 'contemplating a return to British politics'. What could be more slothful? – he never left British politics. He *founded* the Coalition government. He made conditions just right for these lunkheads to take over, and then he fled! He crapped in your lap and ran away. He peed in the empty ice-cream carton that is your life. He did nothing. He did nothing to protect us from these friends of his. This Coalition (and what a word that is – remember the 'Coalition of the Willing'?), this Drones Club, this Castle of Indolence – Tony Blair is part and parcel of it. He is its Creator (how he would love to be called that). His utter sloth made it inevitable. 'Look,' the bums said to each other, '*this* is how to run the country. It's EASY!'

Blair cursed us with the Olympics; the marketers

claimed the Human Spirit was being nourished, when the fact was that the Human Spirit was being diminished, eroded and trampled upon with every hour of Olympic competition, because the Human Spirit loves freedom, and the Olympics, marketing, broadcasting, government and the internet are totalitarian. Some brainwashed jocks ran around a track. And for every one of those muscle-bound gullible tots, there were twenty marketers and fifty company presidents and one hundred BBC journalists using them to sell xylitol and electronic cigarettes to 4.8 billion slobs watching television. 4.8 billion slobs who *must die*, without having their spirits nourished.

Who are the slothful? Is it living up to your potential, to be a marketer?

When there is no work, the concept of sloth gets trickier.

There are headlines this week about 'Mini Work' schemes being hatched in the 'minds' of the Treasury. Mini-work, no work, and finally *unpaid work offered to the destitute*. I have to say this is the final indignity, to a sloth guy. Work is now, finally, meaningless. Everyone is expected to act as though they have work, when very few have work. But you must keep shopping.

Lots of poor people watch *The Wire* because there are a lot of poor people on the show. Who are very highly paid. So everything's tickety-boo.

It's true that the young have no concept of work. Any indication of it is now absent from what little education they get, and it's certainly absent – the *fact* of work – from their major sources of information about the world, television and the internet. There, everyone has money. And every kid in the country now believes that he'll make a million pounds. *Because everyone on television has money.* They believe in Steve Jobs. Ironic last name, isn't it?

One of my young students several years back blazoned his notebook every autumn with the legend THE GREAT BERNIE K_____. But Bernie, what are you planning to be great at? I asked him. Something'll work out, he said every year.

And as for 'Occupy', and other enfeeblements of promise, whatever happened to the real history of the quest for social justice? Whatever happened to socialism? Whatever happened to reading Karl Marx? Oh. The internet.

The Party For The Hole

I live in a city that has been willingly and completely delivered into the hands of marketers. Because so many people make their living here in marketing, and because so many of my fellow citizens have no choice but to blindly follow their dictates, it wouldn't be exactly fair to name it. It's Edinburgh. The marketers have turned Edinburgh from a pleasant European city of benign, contemplative eighteenth-century aspect into a garbage-strewn, vomited-over funfair. They even succeeded in pushing us away from our benign, contemplative eighteenth-century whiskies; whisky no longer exists in Scotland. Our national drink is vodka and we each drink three litres of it an hour. It's a real festival.

Several years ago the marketers decided that since Edinburgh was a city of a certain size, it required trams. Trams were tony. In more ways than one. (A key part of Blairism is the continuous destruction of functioning infrastructure. The people must constantly be off their guard, so that they can be robbed.) The very day this was decided some men came and dug a hole in front of my neighbour's fish shop. They put up weak, cheap plastic barriers around it, and went away after glowering at everybody. They went away for a very long time.

Sloth? Or the necessities of a large and complex civil engineering project being run by hick councillors and marketers instead of engineers?

People got tired of the hole. Little kids could fall into it. It started to get a little bigger, what with rain and erosion and what have you. It was ugly. It held up traffic. And it prevented people from parking outside the fish shop and nimbly skipping inside for Arbroath smokies.

After a year had passed my neighbour and some other merchants of benign eighteenth-century aspect decided to hold a birthday party for the hole. Just to – you know. *Remind* gently the marketers that an actual real hole had been physically dug, as opposed to their limitless interior nothingness. There were balloons and 'Happy Birthday, Hole!' banners. Someone baked a cake. In the middle of the celebrations a truckload of heavy thugs trundled up. They were from Blair Social Engineering plc. They popped the balloons, tore down the sign, threw the cake to the dogs (not to the poor, who were gathering). *They grabbed an innocent old lady and shoved her into the hole!* Then they went away.

Sloth must be preserved. Sloth must be above suspicion.

SLOTH CONQUERS ALL

The time has come to act. I'm going to use *my* sin, sloth, to shut down the other six. This will work. It's got to. Because I want to keep looking out at the river. Without being damned.

Sloth will bring down the bankers. *Is* bringing them down. We will be crawling around on all fours, so it'll be far too much trouble to envy somebody and there'll be no money to be greedy for. I'm going to stuff your head like a pepper with billions of contradictory worries about your diet, so when you do finally trudge to the farmers' market you'll be too scared to buy anything. You'll also be weak with hunger.

Consider pride. Are you proud of yourself? For anyone suffering from pride, I can offer a very simple and effective solution, which I have tried and proven myself. You will be turned into a university lecturer. After a week no one will even look at you. After two weeks no one will be able to remember your name. After three weeks you will start to weep spontaneously at the mere mention of 'literature', 'students', or 'education', and will be contemplating various shameful, secret suicides. By the end of the first term, sloth will have destroyed your pride as surely as Kindle burns books. You will feel like cheap institutional or even industrial toilet paper on a shoe.

Or lust. How slothfully have I admired it. Without participating in it. Enough. But here the World Wide Web is my sword and my gift. (Say, I sound like a pretty energetic fellow. This is temporary, I assure you. The river. The dog.) There seems no longer any need for men and women to desire each other, certainly not to procreate. Civilisation is over, and soon life will be, too. So this is our chance to stop anyone falling in love or even being able to stomach the sight of each other. I give you, *par exemple*, Tumblr: one million billion trillion freakishly animated little tiny boxes. Glimpses into the former biological life of our species, with bikinis, with rubber hoods. With the panties of a sextillion Japanese schoolgirls to the tenth power. With so much unfairness, prejudice, stupidity, with the biggest load of curmudgeonly doubt since the Middle Ages. Tumblr will take over your brain. It will crawl over your mind and face all night, the little pictures like ants in your pants, your synapses. Women will shun you and men will buy you drooling-beer (not a sin, remember?). And no one need ever conceive of another as cherishable, ever again. *Nothing will be cherishable*, or meaningful. Or even recognisable. If you mumbl 'Tony Blair' in your slumbr it sounds like 'tumblr'.

Now I will confess something: I am feeling wrathful toward someone else in this book –

[Enter MR ATTIC, with candlestick.]

But all of this was guesswork, you know. Guesswork is sloth. How could we ever know anything about the truly slothful? The truly slothful have left no records.

Wrath

John Sutherland

DIVINE WRATH

Wrath sometimes tops the list of the seven deadly/ capital/mortal/cardinal sins/vices of the flesh. (I trust, chauvinistically, that it will lead the way in this collection – one likes to see one's name coming first, but, since pride – even in one's favourite sin – goes before a fall, perhaps I hope in vain.)

Dante puts wrath a high-up sixth among the nine infernal circles where the wrathful on earth have their arms and legs torn off eternally, semi-submerged in a noxious swamp which, with all that dismembered meat drifting in it, must resemble the Devil's stewpot. The punishment, as in all the circular houses of pain, is diabolically apt. It would require more than

Paralympic athleticism to be wrathful without limbs. Armless is harmless.

Sin tends to come, as Shakespeare's Claudius (a notable sinner – with 'hectic' raging in his blood) says, not in single spies but in battalions. There are various catalogues of them bundled in the Bible, as in Galatians, where, as the neurotically body-hating Paul lists them:

> Now the works of the flesh are manifest, which are *these*; Adultery, fornication, uncleanness, lasciviousness,/Idolatry, witchcraft, hatred, variance, emulations, wrath, strife, seditions, heresies,/Envyings, murders, drunkenness, revellings, and such like: of the which I tell *you* before, as I have also told you in time past, that they which do such things shall not inherit the kingdom of God.

But it was the Catholic Church in the sixth century under one of the many Gregorys which, by a stroke of disciplinary genius, came up with the number seven (as opposed to the Pauline seventeen, in which wrath comes a measly eleventh).

The cardinal septet was thereby rendered as memorable as all those other sevens – a digit of pre-eminent magical significance in the old pagan numerologies. As, for example, the Seven Wonders of the World, the seven continents, the seven seas, the seven colours of the rainbow, the seven orifices of the body, the seven gods in the Greek pantheon, right the way down to Snow White's seven little people, *Seven Brides for Seven Brothers*, Baldy Brynner's Magnificent Seven, 7/11, and 7UP. The number resonates and sticks in the mind like no other.

Among the reasons one can propose for its being promoted to the top slot among the seven is that wrath is the only sin which one can confidently lay at the Almighty's own door. If He, in other words, has a favourite sin, this must be it. Consider, for example, out of many one could take from Holy Writ, Psalm 7 (inevitably): 'God is a righteous judge, a God who expresses his wrath every day.'

Every day suggests a total lack of any second thought in our Maker when losing His divine rag. It is less that his ire is regularly roused than that it never, if we trust the psalmist, subsides. This daily wrathfulness has always caused theologians trouble and some sophistical fast-footing. Can one imagine, for example, the psalmist enjoining worship of a God who expresses His 'lechery' every day? Or who expressed His 'sloth' every day? Leave that to the semi-demi-divine, Jabba the Hutt.

The only other divine sin charged against Him – with a bit of semantic stretch – is that laid down in His commandment as to the worship of other gods than Himself:

> Thou shalt not bow down thyself to them, nor
> serve them: for I the LORD thy God *am* a jealous
> God, visiting the iniquity of the fathers upon the
> children unto the third and fourth *generation* of
> them that hate me.

'Jealous' can be glossed as 'envious' – one of the worse of the 'active' sins among the deadly seven. And one notes the implicit hint here that infidelity will raise His wrath even against the heretic's luckless great-great-grandchildren, who will suffer without ever knowing why. But can one seriously imagine the Almighty as 'jealous' of such piffling deities as Min, the Egyptian God of Procreation (Moses makes short work of him and all the other Egyptian crew with Aaron's staff tricks, as chronicled in Exodus)?

One should, of course, bear in mind, in regard to that stern Second Commandment, that it, and the other nine, are a second draft after God's wrath has been provoked by the impious Golden Calf. As re-inscribed, the second stony set Moses brings down from Mount Sinai could be called the Angry Ten Commandments. Could there have been more generous rules of desert life, one wonders, on the original slabs that Moses broke to pieces in his rage on seeing that obscene golden thing? A lifestyle more akin to today's Gulf States like Dubai, perhaps – or a little more slack on the question of strict Sabbath

observance and the felonious coveting of one's neighbour's donkey.

My own favourite god (not one to inspire the
slightest jealousy in any rival) is Thot(h), a very minor
pharaonic deity, credited with the invention of writing
and – it is suggested – the patron of scholarly research.
The don among gods, Thot is typically represented
with the head of a baboon, which is not flattering to
those of my profession and is connected, cosmically,
with the moon (as Hegel memorably put it: the owl of
Minerva, wisdom, flies at dusk).

Theologians slip out of the embarrassment of
a wrathful God in a number of ways. One is that
His wrath is inherently different from those of His
creatures. As the Epistle of James puts it: 'For the
wrath of man worketh not the righteousness of God'.
The wrath of God, however, clearly does work that
godly righteousness. It is one of His many mysterious
ways. There is, none the less, something of the slippery
reasoning of *Animal Farm*'s pigs here. If Man is
framed in God's image, why may he not be, when
occasion clearly demands it, wrathful?

Another favourite line of God's apologists is that
Divine wrath is a property exclusive to the Old Testament
Jehovah – a great smiter and constitutionally hasty in
his judgements on mankind (I have always, for example,
thought it small-minded of him to deny Moses, in
what looks like a flash of divine testiness, entry to the

Promised Land after he had trekked virtuously for four decades through the desert wastes). Over time (six thousand years by ancient calculation), it is suggested, God has cooled down. Wrath is an exhausting sin and difficult to sustain over long periods. Unlike revenge, wrath is not something that can be served cold. Hate (sometimes called 'cold wrath') is something else.

The regenerate deity's attitude to wrath is, one is informed by sermonists, embodied in his constitutionally wrath-averse son. The true Christian spirit is – according to the Sermon on the Mount – 'meek', or 'patient', as it is usually glossed in the Seven Heavenly Virtues. The New Testament consistently enjoins wrathlessness. Christ is consistently written up by his disciples as 'gentle' and inhumanly long-suffering, not short-tempered, as are even his most faithful followers (see, for example, Peter's cutting of the high-priest servant's ear, requiring a first-aid miracle by Jesus).

But, one may note, Christ too can have flashes of what can only be called wrath when his goat is got, as it is, royally, by the Pharisees, in Mark 3:

And he entered again into the synagogue; and there was a man there which had a withered hand.

And [the Pharisees] watched him, whether he would heal him on the sabbath day; that they might accuse him.

And he saith unto the man which had the withered hand, Stand forth.

And he saith unto them, Is it lawful to do good on the sabbath days, or to do evil? to save life, or to kill? But they held their peace.

And when he had looked round about on them with anger, being grieved for the hardness of their hearts, he saith unto the man, Stretch forth thine hand. And he stretched it out: and his hand was restored whole as the other.

And the Pharisees went forth, and straightway took counsel with the Herodians against him, how they might destroy him.

As the usually reliable Mark makes clear, Christ performs this miracle not out of charity for the disabled stranger – a lucky bystander – but 'with anger' against his enemies. As the modern idiom puts it, he momentarily 'loses it'. It is not the only time. It is hard to imagine a Saviour who is not pushed beyond the bounds of endurance going to the trouble of constructing a whip of 'small cords' wherewith to drive the money changers from the Temple, overturning their tables in what is surely an extremity of rage. He is, in modern parlance, 'mad as hell' and not going to 'take it anymore'.

Christians (it may be clear I am no longer of their number, although I once was) have always been anxious lest, when Judgement Day comes, they will be confronted by the wrathful God, who in Genesis genocidally destroys all but a handful of his human creation, regarding them, apparently, as of less worth than the paired cockroaches Noah takes aboard for posterity. Or will it be God the Merciful who so loves mankind that he lets his only son be tortured to death for their universal benefit. What mood will the old man be in today? children wonder waiting for a father to come down to breakfast.

One thing the Bible does promise us. In the end days, when the whole game is played out, God and his Son will be very wrathful indeed. As Revelation 6.17 prophesies, when the seventh seal is opened, 'the great day of His wrath' will come and none will be 'able to stand' before it.

No escape from Divine wrath on that terrible day. And we shall all be raised from our graves to face its cruel blast.

RIGHT ROYAL WRATH

'Wrath' has many more (near) synonyms in English than its six companion sins. The terms stress subtle qualitative differences. For example: ire, anger, peevishness, rage, choler, fury, vexation – each of these words calls up a slightly different facial expression and different kinds of action.

Among that lexicon, wrath has what one could call 'grandeur'. The expression it calls up is anger accompanied by regality. The word carries with it a metaphorical crown and sceptre. When, after his outburst against the disobedient (as he thinks) Cordelia, King Lear is cautioned by Kent, he turns on his counsellor with the warning: 'Come not between the dragon and his wrath.' If Shakespeare had made the offended monarch say: 'Come not between the dragon and his peevishness [or whichever of the above synonyms]' the ejaculation would carry a very different and much lesser charge. It would be, in a word, less 'kingly'. Lear is not irked, vexed, irritated, put out, or even angered – but 'wrathful'.

As we later learn, Kent, who is being roared at here, is himself a man with an explosively short fuse. His anger against the infuriatingly cheeky Oswald leads to him ending up in the stocks until his temper cools. But, eminent courtier and nobleman that Kent is, he would not normally describe himself, even in the height of his anger, as 'wrathful'– it's beyond his sin-grade.

The word wrath also carries with it a connotation of social and moral superiority. It validates its possessor as powerful – someone with lightning bolts in their hand (Zeus is the angriest by far of the Olympian gods).

Examples of the hauteur of wrath are easily enough

found, but the following from the Marx Brothers film, *Horse Feathers* (1932) is among the funnier:

> **Secretary**: 'The Dean is furious! He's waxing wroth!
> **Quincy Adams Wagstaff** [i.e. Groucho]: 'Is Wroth out there too? Tell Wroth to wax the Dean for a while.

Were the Secretary to say 'floor-cleaner' rather than a potentate like the Dean, the joke would fall very flat.

Sometimes the word wrath is used specifically for its dazzle-quotient. I have taught intelligent undergraduates John Steinbeck's *The Grapes of Wrath* for forty years. They are perceptive and intelligent readers but I have very rarely known one who could explain what the title actually means – other than that it must mean something very important indeed. 'Wrath' is, of course, rootage wholly unknown to viticulture. Grapes don't grow out of wrath any more than blueberries grow out of lechery or raspberries out of sloth. Arguably the poet who first came up with the phrase got her imagery totally wrong, but Steinbeck uses it just the same.

Steinbeck's title – even if one can't make head nor tail of it – carries even more of a punch if one pronounces the word as Americans do: 'wraahhth', with an open vowel. The British generally close the vowel, producing something homophonous with 'Philip Roth' (a very wrathful novelist indeed nowadays. What does he call God in *Nemesis* (2010)?: 'a sick fuck and an evil genius').

There would be much less punch in a title such as *The Joads: an Okie Tragedy*, more accurate a description as that would be of the actual contents of Steinbeck's novel. The word is often drawn on in this way – to dazzle rather than describe. The best of the *Star Trek* movies is, by general critical agreement (and certainly my own modest Trekkie opinion), *The Wrath of Khan*. The title is, as those who have seen it will testify, a total misnomer. Khan Noonien Singh, as played by Ricardo Montalban, is sneaky, duplicitous, misanthropic and ingeniously sadistic (he does horrible things with extraterrestrial earwigs). Wrathful, in the kingly sense, he is not – his principal beef against Captain James T. Kirk is that he (Kirk) was responsible for the death of Khan's wife and he wants to get his own back. But the title has a mysterious portentousness: 'Khan' is pronounced with the lingering open 'a', which adds to the effect. The title, however inappropriate, carries the kind of heft that grabs a film-goer's attention. One *remembers* it (can anyone but the most fervent fan remember what the first in the franchise was called? *Star Trek: The Motion Picture* – could anything be lamer?).

The screenwriter of *The Wrath of Khan*, the brilliant Nicholas Meyer (called in, at the eleventh hour, to rescue a script that was going nowhere), did not have this title in mind; nor did he know, until it was too late, that it was going to be slapped on his creation by the studio money men. What Meyer had in mind was *The Undiscovered Country* – what Hamlet calls the afterlife. Meyer wanted that title in allusion to the central event of the film, the protracted death of Spock. Creators' wishes should be respected, but Meyer's title would never have worked as well as *The Wrath of Khan*.

Its associations with monarchic dignity make one wonder if wrath should be classified as a sin at all. Like gods, kings are often regarded as being above such pettiness. It could further be argued that wrath is the most necessary of the sins when it comes to the complex business of the making of nations. Put another way, kings make kingdoms, and at crucial moments they need kingly wrath to do so. Whatever the gospels decree, no great kingdoms have been founded on 'meekness'. Romulus and Remus were suckled by a wolf, not a ewe.

Note, for example, how often lions rampant appear on heraldic devices. The animals allegorise the twin properties of regality and savagery. The lion is the king of the beasts – but only in the wild, where he, too, is wild. Wrath is a leonine thing. Edmund Spenser, in one of his digressions in *The Faerie Queene*, describes a parade of the Seven Deadly Sins. This is how the poet pictures wrath (it comes, as in Dante, sixth in the procession):

And him beside rides fierce reuenging *Wrath*,
Vpon a Lion, loth for to be led;
And in his hand a burning brond he hath,
The which he brandisheth about his hed;
His eyes did hurle forth sparkles fiery red,
And stared sterne on all, that him beheld,
As ashes pale of hew and seeming ded;
And on his dagger still his hand he held,
Trembling through hasty rage, when choler
in him sweld.

Spenser's poem chronicles the creation of Albion, or England, and the complex moral mixtures that form its supra-tribal national character. The poem is dedicated to, and nominated for, a monarch: Queen Elizabeth. A lioness among her kind – as the unlucky Philip of Spain discovered.

Anger, allegorised in the lion, is a central ingredient in the mix of primal Albion. In the United Kingdom's Royal Coat of Arms, no fewer than seven of the beasts can be counted – a veritable 'pride' (proudest of all is Leo at the top of the heap, shamelessly displaying his membrum leonis).

One cannot imagine a King of England called 'Richard the Lambheart' – or an England long surviving such a monarch. Royalty has always felt a kinship with the king of the beasts – and, when roused to anger, the most imperiously wrathful of the animal kingdom. Royals can't get enough of them. Richard the Lionheart, in his early career, made do with a modest two golden lions on a red field on his personal display of arms. By the end of his reign, we are told, he was using three lions passant on a red field. Less a heraldic device, one might think, than a gilded, wild-animal park.

What, one must wonder, is the wrath-quotient of more recent British monarchs who still display the traditional lion-embossed coat of arms? Has their wrath, like that of the presiding God of the New Testament, cooled over the centuries? Who knows? In *The Times*, on Jubilee weekend in June 2012, there was, however, the following teasing observation by Ben Macintyre in an article entitled 'What's She Like?':

> Courtiers say that the only time the Queen becomes visibly angry is when someone steps on a corgi's tail. Her father, George VI, had a fiery temper. Queen Victoria could get spectacularly stroppy. But the Queen has gone out of her way to play down any whiff of wrath, or even mild annoyance. When the BBC aired a documentary trailer for *Monarchy: The Royal Family at Work*, edited to make it appear as though the Queen had stormed out of a photo shoot with photographer Annie Leibovitz, the royal lawyers were called in to deny the suggestion that she had walked out in a huff.

Macintyre's words are carefully chosen to leave open the possibility that there lurks, beneath the serenely docile regal mask, the age-old leonine fang and claw ('the whiff of wrath', as Macintyre calls it) – forget corgis.

EPIC WRATH

Languages, linguists jest, are 'dialects with armies behind them'. Epics, the noblest of literary forms, are, one may paraphrase, 'long poems (usually) with great nations behind them'. And, at the heart of the epic, one finds what? Invariably a radioactive kernel of wrath.

Epic deeds would seem to need wrath as, at least, a detonator. What, for example, is the first word in the greatest such poem we have, *The Iliad*? The word is 'wrath' – signalling that at the centre of that great event is the rage of Achilles at the death of Patroclus. This is how the opening goes in Alexander Pope's stately, if bloodless, translation:

> Achilles' wrath, to Greece the direful spring
> Of woes unnumber'd, heavenly goddess, sing!
> That wrath which hurl'd to Pluto's gloomy reign
> The souls of mighty chiefs untimely slain;
> Whose limbs unburied on the naked shore,
> Devouring dogs and hungry vultures tore.
> Since great Achilles and Atrides strove,

Such was the sovereign doom, and such the will
of Jove!

It's clear that Achilles' wrath, as Pope stresses, is
the cause of much carnage and woe – not least the
eventual burning of the topless towers of Ilium. But,
in the longer term, his wrath can be said to bring
about the maritime supremacy of Greece – historically
one of mankind's greatest benefits. A meek Achilles
would have meant, conceivably, Trojan victory and
Troy, not Athens, as ruler of the waves and the cradle
of democracy, philosophy and literature.

As *The Iliad* makes clear, what the Anglo-Saxons
called 'battle rage' – Warrior Wrath – is essential if
you live in embattled times. And very few times have
not been embattled. The wrathless tribe goes under.
The point is made, graphically, in the first surviving
epic of the British peoples, *Beowulf*, which almost
certainly wasn't the first such heroic poem, any more
than Homer's were the first Greek epics. But it is the
earliest that we have.

The hero is fierce – bordering on feral. There is
critical dispute as to what his name means, but general
agreement that 'wolf' is in there somewhere. Beowulf
is consistently described as wrathful before going
into battle. He fires himself up to deal with Grendel
– the nocturnal monster terrorising Hrothgar's Hall,
destroying the civic harmony of the little kingship

– with 'yrre' (ire). Having disposed of Grendel he encounters the monster's vengeful mother as an 'yrre oretta', a 'wrathful warrior', and it's not a pretty picture. But a less than berserkly wrathful Beowulf could not have saved Hrothgar's kingdom. Civilised Denmark, as it now is, would never have come into being without Beowulf's primal act of cleansing wrath, which destroyed, forever, the monstrous forces of darkness.

We have the text of *Beowulf* thanks to an unknown medieval monk in the tenth century who transcribed the poem from oral sources, presumably. He made one or two pious interpolations, but generally – as best we can deduce – he respected the unreconstructed paganism of the original text. His hand must have twitched uneasily, none the less, as he penned the epic tale. Truly observant Christians would have prayed and turned the other cheek to Grendel – assuming they had any cheeks left from last night's flesh-rending visit. But, we deduce, the Seven Heavenly Virtues can only be put into practice after the deadly primal sin of wrath has done its founding work. That, at least, is what poems such as *The Iliad* and *Beowulf* intimate. Wrath – even the wrath of the formidable berserker or the crazed Achilles – is necessary at the right time in the right place.

The great imperial power of our time is the USA. The twentieth century is routinely called 'the American

Century'. Its power, although diminishing, is still paramount among the nations of the world. The US is still a young nation – its bicentenary was celebrated in 1976. Epics tend to be the property of very old nations – typically nations whose imperial power has long gone.

America's search for its epic(s) expresses itself in its obsession with 'The Great American Novel'. One candidate is routinely put forward above all others for that title: Herman Melville's *Moby-Dick*. Central to the novel is Captain Ahab, the skipper of a commercial 'whaler'. Fleets of such ships hunted the northern seas in the mid-nineteenth century for their largest marine mammals. It was not for cat food, nor for the delicacies of the table. It was for oil – the fuel of a great national power on the rise – that the whales were harpooned virtually to extinction. Whale oil was to the USA what coal was to industrial Britain (whose century was also the nineteenth).

Ahab is not, however, a maritime oilman – the equivalent of Daniel Plainview in the 2007 film, *There will be Blood*. Ahab is a man consumed with inner wrath – wrath that he has funnelled as a single shaft of hatred onto a particular white whale, an unnaturally fierce specimen, which earlier wrecked his boat and lost him a leg (replaced with whalebone). The white whale – Moby Dick – has become his great adversary. In a remarkable passage Melville describes Ahab's wrath against it:

Small reason was there to doubt, then, that ever since that almost fatal encounter, Ahab had cherished a wild vindictiveness against the whale, all the more fell for that in his frantic morbidness he at last came to identify with him, not only all his bodily woes, but all his intellectual and spiritual exasperations. The White Whale swam before him as the monomaniac incarnation of all those malicious agencies which some deep men feel eating in them, till they are left living on with half a heart and half a lung. That intangible malignity which has been from the beginning; to whose dominion even the modern Christians ascribe one-half of the worlds; which the ancient Ophites of the east reverenced in their statute devil; – Ahab did not fall down and worship it like them; but deliriously transferring its idea to the abhorred white whale, he pitted himself, all mutilated, against it. All that most maddens and torments; all that stirs up the lees of things; all truth with malice in it; all that cracks the sinews and cakes the brain; all the subtle demonisms of life and thought; all evil, to crazy Ahab, were visibly personified, and made practically assailable in Moby-Dick. He piled upon the whale's white hump the sum of all the general rage and hate felt by his whole race from Adam down; and then, as if his chest had been a mortar, he burst his hot heart's shell upon it.

Meaning in Melville is never easy to pin down, but as I read this, assuming Ahab to be the American par excellence, what it says is that if you dig down what you find – as the essence of America's nationhood – is not something along the lines of 'The Declaration of Independence' ('Life, Liberty and the pursuit of Happiness', etc) but that perverse, destructive and ultimately self-destructive, thing, wrath. That is where it all starts. And, Melville intimates, where it might well finish.

WRATH AND THE ANCIENT WORLD

Wrath was a subject of interest long before medieval sages theologised it as something deadly sinful. One can open the account with Aristotle, whose fundamental proposition is that anger is born in the inherent narcissism – self-importance – of the human species. As he puts it in *Ars Rhetorica*: 'Anger may be defined as an impulse, accompanied by pain, to a conspicuous revenge for a conspicuous slight directed without justification towards what concerns oneself or towards what concerns one's friends.'

(The point will be picked up centuries later by Rousseau, who sees anger as the unwanted child of *amour propre*. Emile, in Rousseau's great tract on education, is counselled to suppress it. It's not a sin: it's selfishness.)

Aristotle goes on to make the shrewd point that anger, as he defines it, necessarily presupposes someone to be angry against. It raises a nice literary conundrum. If he is alone on his island, is it possible for Robinson Crusoe to be angry? Apart from the odd goat, his parrot and the mysterious entity who left the single footprint on the shoreline, there is no person for him to be wrathful against until Man Friday belatedly comes along. Crusoe could, of course, be angry at the supreme being who landed him on the godforsaken (is it?) island (what was it Marlon Brando said of Frank Sinatra, when they were working on the set of *Guys and Dolls*: 'the trouble with Frank is he's angry with God for making him bald'). But the marooned Crusoe fears his God and would not dare offend Him. Lacking human objects, he is no more capable of being angry than – lacking female company – lechery is an option.

Nor, as Defoe describes Crusoe, is he ever angry – although it was in a spirit of manifest rage against his father that he ran away to sea in the first instance. Conceivably God has arranged his long loneliness as a remedy for that aboriginal defiance of the commandment to honour his father and mother. If so He might have preserved the parents to be alive when the chastened son returns. But God's ways are ever mysterious. The Prodigal in the Bible has a father to forgive him: Crusoe, alas, does not when he finally makes it back to Ipswich.

Aristotle goes on to make another shrewd, if controversial, point. Namely that anger/wrath is – in some circumstances – highly pleasurable. The pleasure arises from the fact that anger brings with it the desire for revenge, and vengeance in the mind, like sex in the head (as D.H. Lawrence called it), can be enjoyable and imaginative. More so (where sex particularly is concerned) than the act itself.

Imagined vengeance, says Aristotle, offers the same kind of pleasure as 'images called up in dreams'. This is another area in which Christianity takes a lot of the fun out of life with the stern ordinance 'Vengeance is mine; I will repay, saith the Lord'. Like wrath, it is something which He reserves for His exclusive personal use.

Occasionally – not as often as one would like – it is possible to carry one's wrathful imaginations into execution and do what one fantasises about doing. This, if done well, is even sweeter than the imagined thing. But it needs to done with a certain degree of skill.

In Greek mythology, Atreus's tricking his brother Thyestes into eating his own children for dinner is an example of wrath skilfully put into practice. It is done with the elegance of a winning combination of moves in chess. Creative vengeance of this cunning kind has always been a subject of interest to storytellers. Heathcliff's cold wrath in *Wuthering Heights* takes decades and new generations of victims to bring to its bitter fruition. It is, in a sense, a Heathcliffian work of art rather than an act of revenge.

The film *Seven* (1995) is a more recent exploration of this Aristotelian theme that wrath can be composed, or 'wreathed', into subtle plots and patterns. Two detectives, one old and grizzled (played by Morgan Freeman), the other young and hot-headed (played by Brad Pitt), hunt down a fiendishly clever serial killer (played, chillingly, by Kevin Spacey). Eventually they work out that he is killing his victims – by exquisitely ingenious tortures – sequentially. Each of the victims embodies one of the deadly sins. In a final scene the younger detective is provoked into the climactic seventh sin of wrath, and impulsively kills the killer. Thus the pattern is beautifully complete. The cleverness of it, as much as the sadism, is what makes the film a masterful exploration of its essentially medieval themes.

Classical moralists were, in general, against anger, and sceptical of the perverse pleasures which Aristotle describes. Plutarch's thinking is summed up by the translated title of his treatise, *Of Meekness, or How a Man Should Refrain Choler*. Anger management is the ticket. Plutarch's objection is frigidly rational. Wrath is a 'short madness' which clouds the mind and precipitates rash action, always later regretted. He concedes that 'moderate anger is useful to courage' but moderate anger is, most would say, a contradiction in terms. We would do as well to talk of moderate lechery. It's a sum-zero thing.

Seneca, the grand theorist of the Stoics, is even firmer in his opposition. If Plutarch saw anger as something to be curbed, like an unbroken horse, which might – once 'moderate' – be useful, Seneca was all in favour of exterminating the beast and getting on with life without it. As he writes in *A Treatise on Anger*:

> You have importuned me, Novatus, to write on the subject of how anger may be allayed, and it seems to me that you had good reason to fear in an especial degree this, the most hideous and frenzied of all the emotions. For the other emotions have in them some element of peace and calm, while this one is wholly violent and has its being in an onrush of resentment, raging with a most inhuman lust for weapons, blood, and punishment, giving no thought to itself if only it can hurt another, hurling itself upon the very point of the dagger, and eager for revenge though it may drag down the avenger along with it. Certain wise men, therefore, have claimed that anger is temporary madness. For it is equally devoid of self-control, forgetful of decency, unmindful of ties, persistent and diligent in whatever it begins, closed to reason and counsel, excited by trifling causes, unfit to discern the

right and true – the very counterpart of a ruin
that is shattered in pieces where it overwhelms.
But you have only to behold the aspect of those
possessed by anger to know that they are insane.

Stoics, as Seneca makes clear, have no time whatsoever
for anger. The example of foolishly wrathful Ajax is
routinely cited. Rendered wrathful by Athena, in his
cloudy rage, he thinks he is heroically killing Greeks and
is in fact slaughtering livestock – a lowly occupation.
When he recovers his wits, he is so shame-stricken that
he kills himself. He dies the emblem of the essential
stupidity of wrath.

As rational as the Stoics' disapproval of wrath is, one
can't help but be reminded of Jonathan Swift's jibe that
they are like men who cut off their feet to save on shoe
leather. Even if, as Aristotle claims, it is not necessarily
pleasurable, anger can often be therapeutic: a letting
off of steam. Whether, of course, one would want to
pay for that temporary relief by spending eternity in
Dante's sixth circle, with one's severed limbs floating
alongside one in the cesspit, is something else.

SHAKESPEARE

Dramatists have – like film-makers – always been
attracted to wrath as subject matter because wrath
puts on a good show. It is spectacular. Sloth, on the

other hand, is inherently unspectacular (the only great work of literature based on sloth that I know is Ivan Goncharov's *Oblomov*).

Shakespeare didn't much like the word wrath/wrathful (there are only 71 usages in all his plays, the *Concordance* tells us), but he was fascinated by anger and its place in life. That fascination was highly quizzical and more psychological than moral. It makes for superb theatre.

Where did he pick up his psychological theory? Shakespeare, like his contemporary Ben Jonson (author of *Every Man In His Humour* and *Every Man Out of His Humour*) was wholly persuaded by the 'humoral' explanation of human personality. The theory originated with Hippocrates: as far back as medical history goes. It was refined by Galen, writing in the second century AD. It was, however, in Shakespeare's day, as recent and trendy as the latest wrinkle of psychoanalysis, or primal scream therapy, is to us. Galen's *Book of Elements* (which expounds the humoral theory) underwent its first translation into English by John Jones in 1574.

Humoral theory combines physiology and psychology in elegant patterns. It holds that the body's 'complexion' is the result of subtle confluences of four bodily fluids: bile, phlegm, blood, and melancholy. These connect, symmetrically, with the four elements: earth, air, fire and water. Each of the humours has its organ of residence, or 'seat' in the body: choler (the gall bladder), melancholy (the spleen), phlegm (the kidneys), blood (the heart). Man, as the theory conceives him, is thus a microcosmos, or little world.

Ideally the human personality should maintain the humours, like a well-mixed cocktail, in perfect balance. This is never the case. Subtle imbalances make everyone different. When Shylock, in *The Merchant of Venice*, tells the court:

> You'll ask me, why I rather choose to have
> A weight of carrion flesh than to receive
> Three thousand ducats. I'll not answer that:
> But, say, it is my humour

he does not mean that tearing out Antonio's heart will furnish him amusement but that it is his personal quirk to be irrational about such matters.

Wrath ('choler') is an imbalance of bile. Anger has a special role in the interaction of the humours in that it engenders heat. In consequence it can have a pernicious effect on the other three fluids. Melancholy, for example, can be scorched by choler into the malign condition of 'melancholy adust' – which is the paralytic humoral condition Hamlet finds himself in. The same heat makes the wrathful person 'hot-headed'. Physically the heat manifests itself in red hair (something that descends to the proverbial insult,

'Ginger, you're barmy'). We may assume that in his younger years King Lear, that angriest of monarchs, was flame-haired and flushed of face and, of course, 'hot-tempered'.

Taken metaphorically the humoristic theory is a strikingly accurate descriptor. Its accuracy is witnessed by the fact that we retain, by a kind of semantic inertia, so many of its terms in our everyday speech: 'melancholy', 'sanguine', 'bilious', 'phlegmatic'. 'You've got some gall' we say, without ever recalling Galen.

It would be easy, and convincing, to anatomise the central plot of the film *The Godfather* in terms of Sonny Corleone's too easily aroused 'choler', which leads to his being shot down in the ambush at the expressway tollbooth, Michael Corleone's coldly phlegmatic, years-long scheming and Don Corleone's sanguine view of the quite tolerable minor criminalities of the human race which he will, for his own profit, cater to. Old as the hills as it was, the psychology of Shakespeare's plays in no way renders his drama obsolete.

In his full-length exploration of wrath in *King Lear*, Shakespeare picks up an observation of Aristotle's, namely that the old and feeble are more constitutionally prone to it than the strong and the young. Bile runs markedly with the passing years and age manifests itself by an inability to 'keep one's temper'.

Rage in age links, all too obviously, to impotence of all kinds with the passing years and Shakespeare, in his mid-forties, chose a central character who is by far the oldest in all his dramatis personae. On this rim of human existence, wrath and old age merge into a terminal madness. As Lear begs:

Oh, let me not be mad, not mad, sweet heaven!
Keep me in temper; I would not be mad!

In context 'mad' can mean lunatic or excessively, pointlessly, wrathful. That wrath and madness are closely allied is certified by such contemporary usages as 'Don't get mad, get even' (an instruction sometimes ascribed to Woody Allen) or Peter Finch's bellowing outburst (originally in the film *Network*, 1976, now folkloric) 'I'm mad as hell and I'm not gonna take this anymore'.

King Lear, viewed in its totality, is about a very old man who manifests two of the commonest markers of very old age. He is foolish (in, for example, dividing his kingdom and trusting Goneril and Regan), and he is consumed with uncontrollable and inappropriate rages (as when he exiles the favourite daughter who loves him). He is made to suffer terribly for his twin faults. Finally, after immense pain, he wins through to 'patience' – wrath's opposite 'heavenly' virtue.

Boiled down in this way, *King Lear* would seem to be homiletic. But viewed close up the play is replete with destabilising ironies which defy such easy conclusions. To take just one: in the questionnaire that he puts to his daughters in the first act, the two bad sisters do exactly what is required of them. They flatter the old fool and say, afterwards, that they have recently become aware of 'how full of changes his age is'; of how emotionally fragile he has become. They humour him and get their reward. Cordelia, by contrast, throws back the single word 'Nothing'.

Her answer precipitates a volcanic eruption of rage in her father and a sequence of events which will lead, inexorably, to war, mutilation (Gloucester's eyeballs, most horribly), and a hecatomb of deaths (the whole Lear family among them).

Why does Cordelia not follow the biblical precept ('A soft answer turneth away wrath') and say something pleasing to her father? The Bible shrewdly specifies a 'soft answer', not a 'brutally honest' answer. There will be time enough for honesty later, it is implied, when the occasion is propitious. For the moment, furl your sails and ride out the wrathful storm. The reason, of course, is that Lear's favourite daughter has inherited Lear's vice. Like father like daughter. Her answer is 'angry' – wrathful, even.

Shakespeare is also typically thoughtful and 'modern' on the subject of 'battle rage'. Wars are, after all, not won by the meek: it's a killing business. While it was appropriate for the medieval hero to go berserk against the enemy, it was not for the soldier of Shakespeare's day and Henry V's advice to his troops before storming Harfleur articulates the necessary balances that his men must observe between belligerent ferocity and animalistic brutality:

> Once more unto the breach, dear friends, once more;
> Or close the wall up with our English dead.
> In peace there's nothing so becomes a man
> As modest stillness and humility:
> But when the blast of war blows in our ears,
> Then imitate the action of the tiger;
> Stiffen the sinews, summon up the blood,
> Disguise fair nature with hard-favour'd rage;

What he is saying here is 'pretend to be savages' while being, in your inner selves, civilised human beings. It's a schizoid condition familiar, I suspect, to every military person who has seen 'action' (I haven't). One thinks of David Banner, the mild doctor, who, when the right button is pressed, becomes the Incredible Hulk – the great, green incarnation of wrath. But he isn't really. Underneath he's pussycat David: in witness of which he never, even at his greenest, kills any but the most villainous opponent (viz his most recent showing in *Avengers Assemble*, 2012).

'Anger' is picked up later in *Henry V* in a way that complicates the question of rage in battle. During the great encounter at Agincourt, Henry discovers that the French have infiltrated his lines and killed the unarmed boys in the baggage park. It is, as Fluellen says, 'expressly against the law of arms'. Henry agrees, and it makes him fearfully wrathful. It is now genuine, not simulated, wrath which he invokes:

> I was not angry since I came to France
> Until this instant. Take a trumpet, herald;
> Ride thou unto the horsemen on yon hill:
> If they will fight with us, bid them come down,
> Or void the field; they do offend our sight:
> If they'll do neither, we will come to them,
> And make them skirr away, as swift as stones
> Enforced from the old Assyrian slings:
> Besides, we'll cut the throats of those we have,
> And not a man of them that we shall take
> Shall taste our mercy. Go and tell them so.

The slaughter that ensues is described in Holinshed's *Chronicles*, Shakespeare's principal source for his English history plays:

> Contrarie to [his] accustomed gentleness, [he] commanded by sound of trumpet, that everie man (upon paine of death) should incontinentlie slaie his prisoner. When this dolorous decree and pitifull proclamation was pronounced, pitie it was to see how some Frenchmen were suddenlie

sticked with daggers, some were brained, with pollaxes, some slain with malls, others had their throats cut, and some their bellies panched, sot that in effect, having respect to the great number, few prisoners were saved.

The 'great number' was around 1,500. It is, by any standard, a war crime. A modern Henry might well find himself at the International Court of Justice at The Hague. And the atrocity was perpetrated, on his personal command, because for the first time, as he says, Henry is really angry. 'Wrath', even for supreme leaders, is not a mitigating plea.

Is he culpable? There are other, higher courts. Will Henry go to Dantean heaven, after the necessary spell in purgatory, or will he – by the clamorous demand of all those unarmed French captives killed by his command – end up in the sixth circle?

WRATH AND THE ROMANTICS

For thinking people brought up in the Enlightenment, anger was the enemy of the reason on which that great intellectual reform depended. In 1797, John Fawcett in his *Essay on Anger* put it eloquently:

What a frightful and odious spectacle is the man who delivers himself up to the tyranny of his violent and wrathful passions! ... The man is transformed into a brute, or rather into a fiend and a fury. Detestable sight! Who can behold him without horror? Fly from him; he is a disgrace to human nature. He is now only a fit companion for devils, and ought to be shunned and dreaded by human beings.

One has to suspect that at the root of this disgust was not 'man' but 'men'– demos, that is, wrathful masses set on destroying anything that stood in their way in their demands for fraternity, equality and liberty. Writing in 1797, Fawcett was haunted by the recent American and French revolutions; effusions of gigantic popular anger.

Romantic poets, philosophers and writers tended, on the whole, to a more liberal view of the recent upheavals than Fawcett. But they found themselves in a quandary. No sensible person could be against Enlightenment; no humane individual could approve the terrors which revolution seemed – particularly in France – to bring in its train.

William Godwin articulated this problem in 'On Revolutions' in his *Enquiry Concerning Political Justice* (1793):

The men who grow angry with corruption, and impatient at injustice, and through those sentiments favour the abettors of revolution, have an obvious apology to palliate their error; theirs is the excess of a virtuous feeling. At the same time, however amiable may be the source of their error, the error itself is probably fraught with consequences pernicious to mankind.

Virtuous in its origin, popular anger produces vicious results. Can anger, then, be truly virtuous?

Rousseau, one of the intellectual fathers of the French Revolution, skirted the problem in *Emile* by conceiving anger as a transient symptom of what he calls the 'second birth' of man – adulthood. Adolescents are wracked by testosterone storms. They are what a later age would call 'angry young men' – because they are not yet fully men. So too with society. Popular anger is something that must be lived through as a transitional disturbance on the way forward. A growing-up crisis. The age of fifteen, Rousseau observes, is when this disturbance peaks in the young person:

As the roaring of the waves precedes the tempest, so the murmur of rising passions announces this tumultuous change; a suppressed excitement warns us of the approaching danger. A change of temper, frequent outbreaks of anger, a perpetual stirring of the mind, make the child almost

> ungovernable. He becomes deaf to the voice he
> used to obey; he is a lion in a fever; he distrusts
> his keeper and refuses to be controlled.

Education, the *philosophe* suggests, can handle it. The fifteen-year-old's anger, like most meteorological storms, is short-lived. Batten down the hatches and sit it out.

Shelley, like others of his era who thought seriously about wrath and its political outcomes, was typically conflicted. His most political poem – *The Masque of Anarchy* – is, on the face of it, an outburst of unmitigated wrath against the Peterloo Massacre, in which unarmed working-class Manchester protesters, demonstrating (more or less) peacefully, were cut down by militia men with sabres. The poem ends, rousingly, with the verse traditionally bawled out at the end of Socialist meetings and Labour Party Conferences:

> Rise like Lions after slumber
> In unvanquishable number –
> Shake your chains to earth like dew
> Which in sleep had fallen on you –
> Ye are many – they are few.

Superficially it sounds like a clarion call to arms and bloody revolution. An English equivalent of '*aux barricades, citoyens!*' But this was not what Shelley meant.

His thinking on how the great lions-after-slumber victory could be achieved is expressed more clearly in his long verse drama, *Prometheus Unbound*. The tragic hero who has offended the gods by giving man fire is nailed to a rock-face in the Caucasus, his liver and entrails torn out daily (after nocturnal regeneration), by implacable winged 'furies'. These tormentors are, of course, an allegory of his own inner wrath against the gods' tyrannic treatment of a philanthropist like himself (or Percy Bysshe Shelley). Prometheus frees ('unbinds') himself when he resolves to rage no more, emulating 'a youth with patient looks nailed to a crucifix'. His liberation requires no physical act – no violence – merely a change of mind and a corrected attitude. You can, Shelley believed, *think* yourself free or, as his sceptical wife, Mary (the creator of *Frankenstein*), phrased it: 'Shelley believed that mankind had only to will that there should be no evil, and there would be none.' History gives that fond belief a big 'if only'.

It was a question that perplexed all the canonical Romantics. Revolutions were, viewed from one angle, a good thing in their overthrowing old tyrannies. Revolution was born of enlightenment and rationality: new ways of thinking. But in the acting out of revolution, irrational wrath ruled unchecked. Was that wrath, taking the largest view, a good thing? Was the violence a price worth paying for the ultimate good of humanity?

Like Shelley, Keats cleaved to wise passivity. In *The Fall of Hyperion* the giant race of Titans are vanquished by the upcoming Olympians. The defeated Gods concede their supremacy, wrathlessly, for the reasons expressed by the Titan Oceanus, God of the Sea, contemplating his conquering successor, Neptune:

> 'tis the eternal law
> That first in beauty should be first in might:
> Yea, by that law, another race may drive
> Our conquerors to mourn as we do now.
> Have ye beheld the young God of the Seas,
> My dispossessor? Have ye seen his face?
> Have ye beheld his chariot, foam'd along
> By noble winged creatures he hath made?
> I saw him on the calmed waters scud,
> With such a glow of beauty in his eyes,
> That it enforc'd me to bid sad farewell
> To all my empire.

It is beautifully said. But it is hard to imagine Hitler or Stalin handing over power to aspirant rivals on the ground that they were more pleasing to the eye and damn good surf-boarders.

Most radical, most daring and most persuasive in his views on wrath was William Blake. He was also, in life, the Romantic poet most deeply involved in actual revolutionary activity. For Blake wrath is personally and historically necessary because it can liberate, if properly applied. It was what dynamite was to its inventor Alfred Nobel, a constructive force by virtue of its destructive potential. Most importantly it could shatter those chains which the overoptimistic Shelley thought would melt like dew if only minds could be changed. For Blake the chains ('mind-forged manacles') which bind the mind were the most pernicious of all. 'The tigers of wrath are wiser than the horses of instruction', he grandly proclaimed. Horses were everywhere harnessed – nobody rode the tiger. 'I must create a system or be enslaved by another man's', he also famously declared. Wrath was one of the ways of reaching that independence.

There was, Blake believed, nothing rebellious in it. Indeed, it was a religious duty: 'The wrath of the lion is the wisdom of God.' Most interestingly, Blake believed that repressing wrath brewed self-destructive psychic poison. Or, as he put it in his *Songs of Experience*:

I was angry with my friend:
I told my wrath,
my wrath did end.
I was angry with my foe:
I told it not,
my wrath did grow.

Blake's approval of wrath is the bridge to modern attitudes and thinking about it. They have changed drastically. Since the great uncertainties of the early nineteenth century we have, it's fair to say, come to terms with anger. The growth of psychology as an area of research and medical treatment has been instrumental in this process.

Anger is, as most of us have now come to think, a constituent and necessary part of what is called 'emotional intelligence'. Not a 'short madness', but necessary to the precariously balanced state of sanity. I take the following (much abbreviated) from the website of a highly regarded firm, Harley Street Psychotherapy, which specialises in 'anger management':

> Anger is a fundamental human emotion that all people have. It is usually triggered when we have felt attacked or mistreated or perhaps when our values and beliefs have been challenged... Anger is both necessary and useful and at its best can be an appropriately assertive response to certain life situations. It can support a healthy refusal to be treated badly and be a protective instinct towards one's family and loved ones. However, if managed badly it can be destructive... When working with anger the purpose is to find the most creative and positive use for it in situations where it can be appropriately employed and to address those

situations where the purpose of anger gets lost and it becomes a more negative and destructive influence.

In other words, as the popular song once put it, it ain't no sin. But it's taken 1,400 years to reach that conclusion. And, who knows, perhaps we're wrong.

The Modern Psyche

Ali Smith

I mean, it's not that I don't believe in subtext, I say.

You look up from your muesli.

Because to tell the truth I probably believe in subtext more than I believe in God, I say.

You shake your head.

I have absolutely no idea what you're talking about, you say.

This is understandable since ten minutes ago I said good morning and you said good morning back, and five minutes ago I asked did you want coffee today and you said yes please, and until now those are the only things we've said out loud. Somewhere across town I can hear a bell ringing; it's Sunday, so we're having late breakfast before we go to the garden centre. You will probably spend breakfast time, as usual, winnowing your muesli with your spoon to find the little bits of dried fruit in it. When you find one, you push it to one side of the bowl and eat round it, tipping the milk towards you. After every breakfast, there is always a little mound of small dried fruit chunks stuck to each other, stuck to the side of your bowl. You look like you slept well. I didn't, though, because last night, about an hour before we went to bed, you accused me of trying to kill you.

So.

What I'm talking about, I say, is. I know there is a psychoanalytic theory which states that beyond the mere appearance of us as benign humans in benign relationships with other benign humans, underneath it all nothing about us is benign at all and all we really want is to do malevolent violence to people, most of all to the people we're supposed to love and so on.

Yes, you say.

But I did not leave that piece of orange peel fermenting in the waste bin in the bedroom because I want to kill you, I say.

You put your bowl down on the table and you laugh.

I swear, I say. I swear with all my heart.

It doesn't make any difference how much you swear or what you swear on, you say.

I know I couldn't do a thing like that, I say. I know I could never want to hurt you.

It doesn't make any difference how much you think you know about yourself, you say.

Last night you found the coil of peel – from an orange I ate about three weeks ago – in the bin in the bedroom. With a few discarded pages of notes from your psycho course lightly roofing it and with a wet tea bag curled inside it, it had spent those few weeks growing a web of mould up the sides of the bin that looked, when we discovered it, as complex, layered, tunnelled and dimensional as the model Fritz Lang uses for the animation scenes of the city in the film *Metropolis*. You are allergic to mould. It is why you can never ever be given penicillin, a fact engraved with acid on one of the neurological platelets in my brain (or whatever the places where we store knowledge in our brains are called, I don't know what they're called) in case I ever have to tell it to a doctor who might be treating you in a situation where you're unconscious. You had been complaining for days about the strange smell in your room. I couldn't smell anything, maybe something a bit high and sweet. You kept saying the word citric. You had been having a bit of trouble breathing at night. Last night you lifted the bin and dislodged the papers to reveal the mould.

That's when you accused me of trying to murder you.

Not consciously, maybe, you said. But it did have

the potential to do me harm. So unconsciously, subconsciously, you meant me harm.

I did not, I said.

I said the word not a lot. I cleaned the bin out with antibacterial disinfectant, rinsed it three times and dried it and put it back under the desk. We went to bed. I didn't sleep much. I couldn't, I was too conscious of consciousness to.

Now, over your muesli, you say much the same thing again. You use words like subconscious and unconscious. You squeeze the congealed fruit to the side of your bowl with the teaspoon.

I wish you wouldn't do that, I say.

Do what? you say.

That thing, with the fruit, I say.

Such hostility, you say. Then you raise your eyebrows at me and you laugh.

There are some knowledges about others and ourselves that we just can't handle, you say. That's why we have subconscious and unconscious selves. And you can't rule out the actions of your subconscious.

How could my subconscious want to kill you? I say. Why?

Envy, you say.

Envy? I say. But I don't envy you. I don't envy anything about you.

Mm, you say.

It's just laziness, I say. It was just forgetfulness. I

put a piece of peel in the bin, we forgot to empty the bin, and look what happened.

Look what happened, you say.

What would I want that you've got? I say. It's not like you've got a swimming pool and a Porsche, not that I'd want those things even if you had them. And anyway, we share everything. Don't we?

Envy's only partly about wanting what the other person's got, you say. Mostly it's about wanting the other person not to have what he or she's got. And there's envy in all of us.

I don't envy a single thing about you, I say.

You do, you say. You can't help it. You probably envy me for knowing about the workings of the subconscious when you don't.

I envy you for knowing about envy? I say.

Yep, you say.

You open the newspaper at an article in it about one of the Brit art artists, the woman whose stuff I quite like but you don't.

Oh God, you say and close the paper again.

I do so know about the subconscious, I say.

Why is she always in all the papers? you say. She can't even draw.

And anyway, I say. If there's envy in all of us. That means you must envy me too, then. If I envy you.

Yeah, but it's not me who left a piece of rotting stuff, something which could do you serious harm if you breathed anywhere near it, in the bin in the room where you sleep, though, is it? you say.

It was an ACCIDENT, I say.

There's no such thing, you say.

Since you started that course you talk the most appalling rubbish, I say.

See? you say.

See what? I say.

You envy me doing my course, you say.

I do not! I say.

I fold my arms. You fold the newspaper and throw it away from you onto the couch.

Then it is eight hours later. You've looked up the newspaper's online site and read out some of the horrible things people have written in the online comments thread about the artist you don't like, because lots of people are as annoyed by her as you are and that makes you happy. We've been to the garden centre and bought three roses, we've planted them in some new tubs and redone some hanging baskets, I've cut the grass and you've done some tidying things round the borders, and I am still saying the words *I don't*.

Anyway, it's okay, you say brandishing the rose cutters. I intend to treat it as benign envy. There's such a thing. Even though, if I wanted to, there's plenty reason for me to see it as malicious.

You can make your own supper, since I'm so potentially malicious, I say.

As it happens, I do make supper and we eat it and drink half a bottle of wine each and tease each other a bit more and it's nice, it has the appearance and the trappings of a very nice evening.

But all afternoon it has been disturbing me, and now all through a Sunday night of not very good TV nothing can distract me from the sense, somewhere at the back of everything, that I might have done or might be doing something harmful without knowing, and that something I didn't even realise I'd done might have turned out to be harmful. All night I worry, without letting it show, about things I could be feeling and not knowing I'm feeling.

That night in bed I put my book down and turn towards you. You are reading one of your psycho books. Anne Gray, *An Introduction to the Therapeutic Frame*.

Tell me about it, I say.

Got to have it finished by Wednesday, you say.

No, I mean envy, I say. How we all have it.

Um, you say.

Please, I say.

You keep your eyes on your book.

I mean, it's a deadly sin, isn't it, one of the deadly sins? I say.

I can never remember what they are, you say.

No, me neither, I say, though I remember when I was small getting them mixed up with the Ten

Commandments. They're all a bit average-sounding. It's like, you expect killing people to be one and then it isn't, and instead they're all about eating too much, or, one is sloth, isn't it? Kind of unexpected, I mean deadly seems a very strong word for being a bit lazy. They're all things that don't seem that deadly when you look at them.

Like that piece of peel, you say.

Don't, I say. *Please.*

I turn away from you in the bed and put my hands over my face. I am full of guilt. Or is it shame? I can't tell. I don't actually know what the difference between those two things is.

I hear you close your book, hear something that sounds like you putting it on the bedside table.

Okay, you say. Where would you like me to start?

At the beginning, I say through my hands.

Good, you say, because the thing about envy is, it starts almost immediately after we're born.

I turn back to you with my hands still over my face.

That can't be true, I say.

In the beginning you say, was the Word, and the Word was Klein. Here's a bedtime story for you. There was once a psychoanalyst who –

Ha, I say, who, like all psychoanalysts, had the word anal at the heart of his occupation.

And it's a she, not a he, you say.

Very sorry I'm sure, I say.

Subconscious hostility concerning women in power, you say.

Oh for fuck sake, I say.

There was once a psychoanalyst, you say, whose quite persuasive and very influential theory was that even at its earliest stages love is a matter of anxiety, and that a very small baby at the breast will already be ricocheting between love and hate.

Oh but that's ridiculous, I say. Babies don't feel hate.

But you think they feel love? you say.

Of course they do, I say.

And if they can feel love...? you say.

Ah, I say.

She thought, you say, that the first thing we ever envy is the breast that feeds us, precisely because we are not in control of it, because it comes and goes on its own terms, and it may not always satisfy us, stuff like that. And the first thing we want to do, when we experience the breast not giving to us or realise that the breast can be taken away, is bite the breast that feeds us.

Well, I wasn't breast-fed, I say, so it definitely doesn't apply to me in any case.

It applies to all of us, whether we were raised by breast, bottle or wolves, you say. According to Melanie Klein, the first inkling of destructive impulse is felt right there, at the breast. Tiny babies want to destroy the breast.

That's insane, I say.

She talks about how there's the good breast and there's the bad breast, you say. And unless we're lucky, and get the good breast and the bad breast pretty evenly, so that the good breast provides fulfilment and the possibilities for the formation of gratitude with equal measure to the anxiety caused by the bad breast, then our personalities will, uh, develop accordingly. At least I think that's what she means, I'm not sure, because all I can really remember apart from the thing about there being a good breast and a bad breast is that she spends a lot of the essay she wrote about it griping about how suspicious she is of her clients.

Why? I say.

She thinks they're all envious of her, you say.

Ah, I say. So. Unless we get the good breast, or enough of the good breast, we'll develop like wolves?

No, you say. There's no wolves.

You said wolves, I say.

Why are you on about wolves? you say.

It's not me who mentioned wolves, it's you, I say.

Then I start to wonder if maybe I imagined it that you said anything about wolves. Maybe you didn't. You start explaining about how and why babies get so furious. I zone out of this explanation because I am imagining being suckled by a wolf. I think about the fur, the warmth of the short hair of the belly of the wolf, or would it be shaggy? And the doggy smell, and the nipples like a dog's or a cat's all in a row. Then I wonder how many nipples female wolves actually have. They definitely have more than two. Say they have four, or is it six, or eight, would that mean that half the nipples they have would be good nipples and the other half would be bad nipples? Would one side, one row, be the good side and the other be the bad side?

Then I think about what it would be like to suckle a wolf, or maybe a litter of wolves. There would be fights, if there were a lot of wolf cubs waiting to suck and the mother was human and had just two nipples. Then I wonder if the cubs who were suckled by the bad breast would turn out bad and destructive, biting the faces of babies in prams like urban foxes in the papers, and if wolves suckled by the good breast would turn out good, like dogs, a bit tame. Then I begin to wonder whether good equals tame and bad equals wild.

While you talk about the destructive impulse, I imagine being surrounded by four or five small cubs all nipping at my chest and stomach, or nipping the stuffing out of the cushions on the couch, or the pillows on this bed, because they're having to wait their turn. Then I look down at my own chest. I wonder which is which, the good one and the bad one. Then I hear you talking about how, deep in this destructive impulse, there's also a creative impulse. When I hear this my good/bad chest fills with hope.

So me putting the peel in the bin, even subconsciously, might have been a creative act? I say.

Are you only ever interested in yourself? you say.

No, I say.

But I feel ashamed again. I turn over in the bed.

What? you say. What's the matter?

Nothing, I say.

No, come on, you say. What? Tell me.

I'm ashamed, I say.

What about? you say.

That I don't know the difference between guilt and shame, I say.

It's not why I turned over at all but I don't want to say out loud that it was hurtful, what you just said about me always only thinking about myself. (Also, I'm still mortified at myself for getting the gender of that psychoanalyst wrong. That was really politically incorrect of me.)

I'm ashamed because I'm an adult, I say. I live in the real world. And I have never once thought about the difference between shame and guilt before.

Self-denigration, you say. Classic reaction of the envious person. In denial. I-am-not-worthy. Classic. Textbook.

Just because you know a lot about envy doesn't make you always right, I say inside my head.

Out loud though I don't say anything. I feel you reach across to the other side of the bed. I hear you open your book again. Then I work out, from the glow on the ceiling from your screen, that no, it's not your book, you're online.

Two hundred and forty comments, you say. And most of them negative. Ha.

I don't really want to listen to you reading out any of the comments. In fact, I tell myself that if you do read even a single one of them out, I will end our relationship here. Here and now, I'll decide to leave you. I imagine the long comments thread snaking down the screen. I wait. I hold myself tense for a fragment of the vitriol of a nation. But you don't read anything out. Ten minutes of silence later the glow on the ceiling cuts out and you toss the screen to the end of the bed and turn and kiss me between the shoulders.

Night, you say. God bless.

God bless. I lie there thinking up a rejoinder about how the word bless is related, in French anyway, to the word for a wound, which is something I've known since I did French at school.

I think I remember that the history of saying *God bless* comes from the Black Plague years, when people would say bless you to people who sneezed as a good-luck charm against the plague, since one of the signs of going down with it was sneezing, like in the children's rhyme, atishoo, atishoo, we all fall down. I start to wonder about when it was that bless swapped meanings between wound and blessing. I wonder if it meant, at any point, *God wound you*, and whether maybe the people who wished the people who sneezed well were actually under the surface wishing them ill.

I get a whole sentence ready to say: *isn't it interesting about bless being so close to the French, about wounding, blessure, I don't mean anything by it, I just think it's interesting*. But then I can't say it because I can feel from the way you're breathing that you're asleep and I don't want to wake you, you've got work in the morning too and it wouldn't be fair.

I get some sleep that night, though, so things are a little better the next day. In fact I don't think about envy once, or about the peel or what happened with it, all through breakfast and the drive to work and the first bout of admin at work.

But at about eleven that morning I find myself looking – and not as surreptitiously as I might have hoped I'd do such a thing – at the chests of the women round me, and thinking to myself, if that's the good one, then does that make the other one the bad one?

I shake my head. It panics me that the thought has been there inside me – that even though I thought I *wasn't* thinking about envy, when I looked at my workmates' chests there was the thought, inside me all along, coiled, fermenting invisibly.

At lunchbreak I look down at my own chest. I haven't had children, so does that mean neither of my breasts is bad or good? Or are they bad or good regardless? And does one good breast and one bad breast also translate for all the other things we have two of, or is it only breasts? Is there also one good hand and one bad hand, one good foot and one bad foot, leg, ear, eye, lung, nostril, ovary, kidney?

It's lucky, I think, that we *have* more than one breast. What if human beings had been born with just one, like a Cyclops breast in the centre of the chest?

Then I begin to worry about my heart. I only have one. Is it a good heart or a bad heart, could it be a heart that has known badness since the first day it started beating? And my brain, is it a good or a bad brain? Isn't there a theory about sides of the brain? One side good, one side bad? And my genitals? They're plural, but I only have the one set. And do men have one bad testicle and one good testicle, or is it only women it applies to?

That night when we get into bed I am at least a little more prepared. You are still reading the Gray book. I lean over towards you.

Did you know, I say, that, same as there's the good breast and there's the bad breast, if there are two people in a bed and they both tell a bedtime story like you did last night about the good breast and the bad breast, then one of them is the good person and one of them is the bad person?

Oh really? you say not looking up from your book.

It starts at childhood, I say, and it's about

nourishment. It's about which person is the most fulfilling in the telling of a story.

You close your book and look at me seriously.

Are you making fun of me? you say. You'd better not be.

It's formative, it's about formation, I say. If the story gets taken away, or doesn't nourish the child properly, or makes the child crazy because the child realises that at any point the story can be removed, or unfinished, or might not satisfy, or might not meet his or her needs, then all hell will break loose afterwards.

Are you challenging me to a story competition? you say. And since when was story competitive anyway?

Since people realised how powerful it is, I say. And it's not that it's competitive as such, it's that telling stories is one of the only tools we have for dealing with envy.

How is story a tool against envy? you say.

Well, I say. Consider the old pictures of Invidia.

Of what? you say.

Invidia, I say, the original envy, the name for the personification of envy, which as a word literally means looking off to the side, or looking askance. Invidia, when she's pictured, has a snake wrapped round her arm, held out like a hand waiting to bite the hand it shakes. Consider the personifications of envy as someone with a snake coming out of his or her mouth like a long tongue, but then that snake darts back and strikes its own person in the eyes. Consider Dante, who wrote that envious people walk round in hell with cloaks made from lead on their backs and with their eyes sewn shut with leaden wire.

Yes, but how does any of that make story a tool against envy? you say again.

It helps us see, I say. Seeing is the opposite of envy. Envy is all about not seeing.

Have you been looking up Wikipedia? you say.

Listen, I say. Once there was a really beautiful person who everybody was envious of because she was so beautiful and because she meant no harm to anybody. Her beauty was a bit of a problem, actually, because it meant that no one would ask for her hand in marriage, they thought she was actually too close to being a goddess. This meant that goddesses were jealous of her, especially Venus, who got fed up of men mistaking this person for a goddess, and also was furious with the girl for leaving a piece of fresh orange peel one day as an offering on one of her altars.

Ha, you say.

Yes. It had been all the girl had had with her, in her pocket, when she was passing the temple, I say, and she had very much wanted to leave a sacrifice. Anyway Venus was offended by the peel, but really by the beauty – and the harmlessness – of the girl, and she sent her son to sort this girl out, she said to Cupid: go to that girl and peel back the skin over her heart and insert into that heart this piece of peel she left on my altar, so that badness will ferment in her heart and from now on she'll be blinded to goodness and only capable of falling in love with the bad in people.

I see, you say.

Okay, Cupid said, and off he went, holding the piece of peel out in front of him as he flew, still fresh, still smelling slightly of the fruit it had once protected. But when he saw the girl he fell in love with her, he couldn't not, because she was so good and incapable of doing a single mean thing, consciously or otherwise. So he threw the peel over his shoulder and it fell to earth and landed in somebody's bin without the people who lived there knowing anything about it. And you may think you've heard of a phrase, *pale with envy*. In fact, the real phrase is *peel with envy*, because that piece of peel landed in the world of mortals and spread Venus's envy across the universe like mould.

Yeah, you say, but apart from you adding your cutesy reference about the bit of peel, this is just the story of Cupid and Psyche.

Oh, I say (annoyed). You know this story?

And then the sisters get jealous of their pretty sister sleeping with a god, you say, and tell her how her new husband is really a huge snake and that she ought to kill it, and give her a knife to do it with.

Maybe, I say, but wait, wait, the bit of the story that's most important comes way after that, after she loses Cupid, when she becomes Venus's slave and Venus gives her those tasks where first she has to sort millions of different kinds of seeds so small you can hardly see them, in a seed pile as big as a mountain, into all their separate kinds, and then when she's done that she's got to go and get a handful of wool off a murderous sheep that kills humans, and then she's got to bring back a goblet of water from a legendary river that's across a mountain range impossible to reach, and then, once she's done those, Venus says, she's still got the biggest task of all, she's got to go down to the underworld and bring back the beauty of the queen of the underworld. In a box.

That's not the important bit of that story, you say. The important bit, the most interesting thing in that story is how much it's about what's veiled and what's seen, what's known and what's not.

No it isn't, I say.

The whole point of that story is that Cupid won't let her see his face, you say. She's not allowed to know she's sleeping with a god. And when she brings back the box with the beauty in it, if I remember rightly, she's been told on no account is she to open it, the box, and look at the beauty. But she does, doesn't she? And then what happens? She loses consciousness. Because that's the price for looking too closely, if you're mortal.

Yes, I say, uh huh, I know –.

There's always got to be something, you say, between us and the truth.

But, I say. But. Then, but then, she gets brought back to consciousness and they all live happily ever after because she gets made into a goddess so it's all okay.

You start laughing.

A murderous sheep, you say.

Yeah, but let me tell it properly, I say.

And how exactly does this story defeat envy anyway? you say.

If you'd let me –, I say.

Peel with envy, you say. Ha. Here's a story about what happens when you peel the skin off envy. Here's a new old story for you. The following is … the testimony of a man who threw himself off the top of the building in the middle of town – the building that used to be Borders bookshop, before Borders folded.

The Borders in town? I say. A man jumped off it? Is it a true story?

As true as they come, you say.

But I'm not finished telling *my* –, I say.

You turn over beside me, shunt yourself on top of me as heavy as a stone slab and put a hand over my mouth. Then, putting on a spooky deep voice, as if you've changed into someone else, you say:

Listen.

The day I read that book by him something changed for me forever.

I remember it with an anger so hot that it turns me cold. It was an ordinary day, like any other. It was evening. I thought I'd read for a bit. I used to like reading a book. So I was sitting in the best chair in my house, my chair. I loved my house, I loved my job, I was a happy person with lots of friends and a loving family, back in those innocent days.

I sat in my chair with a book I'd always thought I should probably read, one of those books everybody was supposed to read, like *Moby-Dick* or *Middlemarch*. So I opened it and started reading: *my purpose is to tell of bodies which have been transformed into shapes of a different kind.*

I was such an innocent. I read about thirty pages. Change after change happened, like you'd expect, a god becoming human, a woman turning into a tree, another into a clump of reeds, a boy became a swan, a girl became a bear etc, and I began to think about which of the changes in my own life had not been ones I'd particularly wanted, I sat through all the visitations from gods and I began to wonder if I'd ever had a visitation and just not known it. I was getting tired of all the changes. I decided I'd read to the end of the chapter then I'd stop.

The last three or four pages I read of it were about a goddess who wants to infect a girl with envy because of something unresolved in their past. So the goddess goes to visit a being called Envy who lives in a filthy cave, to get Envy, who is a powerful monster, to poison the girl *noisome slime* the cave is *hidden away* in a place where there's no sun *fireless* it was a *shrouded* place anyway I was reading about how the goddess knocks on the door of the cave *busy at a meal of snake's flesh* and the story out of nowhere twined me round and as easily as anything, as easily as if I really didn't matter, cancelled my whole existence *half-eaten corpses dragging steps sickly pale* like my job didn't exist, like the work I'd done that morning meant nothing in the world, nothing that would last anyway, like no amount of me sitting correcting the copy on the websites of the companies who employed me to keep their use of the English language simple would ever make any difference to anything *lean and wasted* like the house I'd bought and lived in and we'd filled with all the things you're supposed to have in a house, that my hard work, years of hard work, had made possible, was a waste of *squinted horribly discoloured and decayed* like for the first time a story *of a greenish hue dripped venom* read me and when I looked up from that book I could hardly move, it took everything I had just to get myself up out of that chair.

I lit a fire in the grate in the front room. It was a stupid thing to do because we had that chimney blocked up five years ago. See what he made me do? He made me nearly burn down my home. He made me ruin our front room. Anyway I burnt it and it gave me pleasure to. But even so I couldn't sleep that night, and not just because of the smoke damage and the kids crying and my wife going on about what I'd done to the curtains.

The day after, I went to a bookshop. I'll get a new book, I thought. By someone else. I'll read another one. But every book in the bookshop was tainted, like I was standing in a chemist's cupboard surrounded by skulls on bottles with gouged-out eyes. I stood in the Classics section. This bookshop had three copies. Three copies! I took one copy of that book off the shelf. I came towards the counter as if I were going to buy it, the way you do, in a bookshop. Then in front of the bookseller, I ripped that book in half. I dropped both pieces on the counter and turned and walked out. I did not offer to pay.

But only twenty yards down the road the good feeling had faded. So I went to another bookshop, the one on the High Street, and checked the sign by the stairs to see which floor their Classics department was on.

Soon the bookshops in town all knew who I was. Soon I had to start going to London because in London no one knew me, yet. I got five copies under my jacket once in Foyles on Tottenham Court Road without anyone knowing and there's a litter bin round the corner on the way to Soho, I dropped them in where they belonged, one after the other, with the putrid leavings of an average day in London. But the relief didn't last, because all over the world there were so many copies. I lost sleep. No, *he* lost me sleep. And *he* lost me my friends. My wife blamed me, she said it's Ovid Ovid Ovid all the time, all the time going on about a dead Latin writer, give it a rest. Me give it a rest! I said. It's not me. It's Ovid. Tell Ovid to give it a rest. Then I'll give it a rest! My wife got custody. That judge was biased – in Ovid's favour. It's Ovid they should ban from picking up the kids at school. It's Ovid they should serve with their exclusion orders.

There was a time when I could still get some sleep by telling myself about how he got exiled. It made me happy that he'd been made miserable, sent away from the home he loved so much. I bet that Black Sea got its name from the black day he came anywhere near it.

I went into the last bookshop left in town that would let me through its doors. Everything in my life was sludge now. I went up the escalators, went through the door marked PRIVATE, punched the bookseller who tried to stop me, kicked in the last of the doors at the top of the stairs and stepped onto the roof.

Some people said afterwards I jumped to see whether I'd turn into a bird.

Bird be damned.

I jumped because Ovid was on my back.

And even as I stepped out of the sludge into

nothing, over the edge, even as I felt the thin air slap me about and the ground come up to meet me, I knew it wasn't worth it. Some things will never ever change.

I'll never be rid of him. He'll never be rid of me.

And that, you say in your own voice, is that.

You lift yourself off me.

Oof, I say.

The relief is immense. You lie on your back on your own side of the bed. You are yourself again.

Ovid, you say. A great source for envy. One of the original sources.

Ovid envy, I say. Like penis envy?

Ooh, you say. I like that.

Do you? I say.

I fill with the pride of having said something clever and at the same time I realise that you're full of pride yourself and that it's because you think your story's blown mine out of the water.

God, you say. Look at the time.

You lean back over and kiss me very sweetly.

I know you didn't mean it, you know, you say. About the orange peel. I know you'd never want to hurt me.

Thank goodness, I say.

In as much as we can ever know for sure, you say.

I don't say anything.

We never need to worry about it again. And that's the last word on it, you say.

You wink at me. I nod and smile. You reach over and switch the reading light out, kick *An Introduction to the Therapeutic Frame* to the bottom of the bed where it falls off onto the floor.

We settle into our usual position for sleeping.

I turn over in the bed, then I turn over again.

No matter which way I turn I can still feel the weight of you on me, even more so in the absence of you.

I lie on my back, my arms folded, my hands each holding one of my own breasts. I think of that man throwing himself off the top of the bookshop.

How selfish. Even if a life story *was* so heavy on someone's back that it made him or her do something like that, someone else still has to clean things up, pick up the mess afterwards.

But your story has partly been about exactly that, I think. Your story has been so clever. It suggests that it isn't the end, that there is no end. There's something dependable in that.

When I'm as sure as I can be that you're asleep, I put my head next to your pillow. I put my mouth close to your ear and I say the following so far under my breath that I almost can't hear it myself.

It's the ants who come to help her sort out the impossible mountain of seeds. Millions of ants just come, from nowhere, and sort the millions of seeds, and in half an hour the impossible job is done. And it's a reed by the river who whispers to her that she doesn't need to go anywhere near the murderous sheep, and that if she just takes a walk past the prickly bushes which the murderous sheep eats the flowers off, she'll be able to pick a big matted handful of wool off the prickles and give that to Venus. And it's an eagle who helps her get the water from the Styx, it flies down to where she's sitting hopeless on a mountain ledge, takes the cup in its beak, flies away, then flies back again with the full cup. And as for your beauty, queen of the subconscious, I take the lid off it and look at it every day and every night. I do not look askance. And I am not immortal. You are beautiful, and I, mere mortal, see it every time, and I never lose consciousness at seeing it.

Not a flicker of a lid or lash; not the slightest shift in your breathing; you haven't heard a word I've said.

That means the last word's mine.

Good.

Gluttony

Martin Rowson

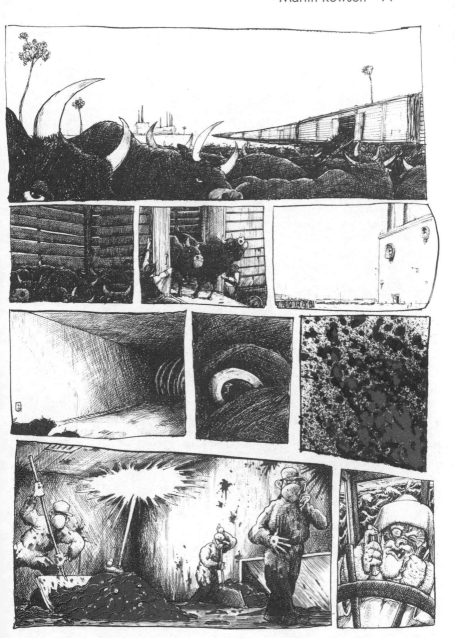

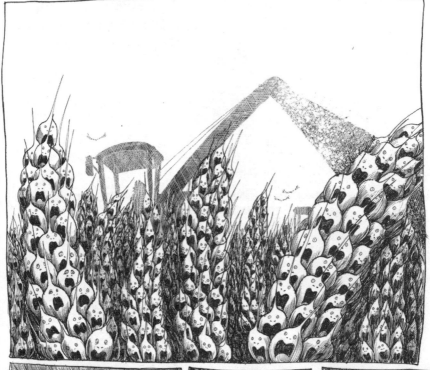

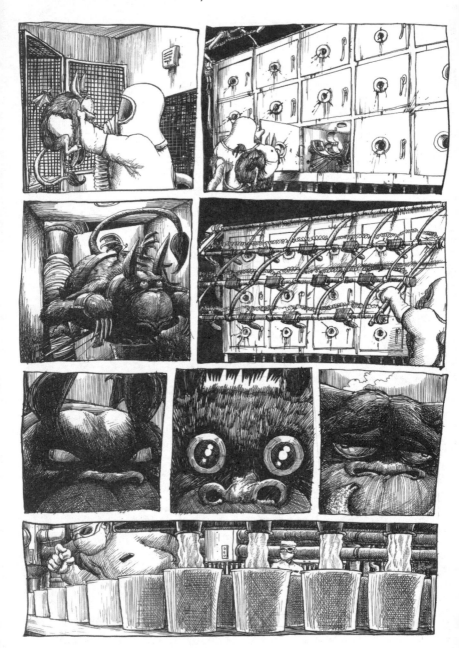

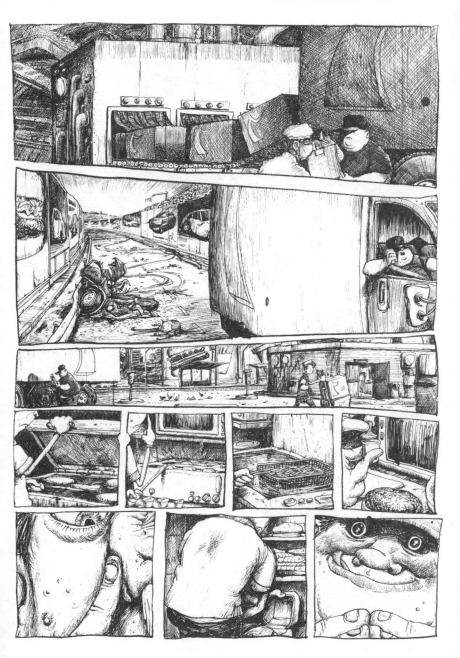

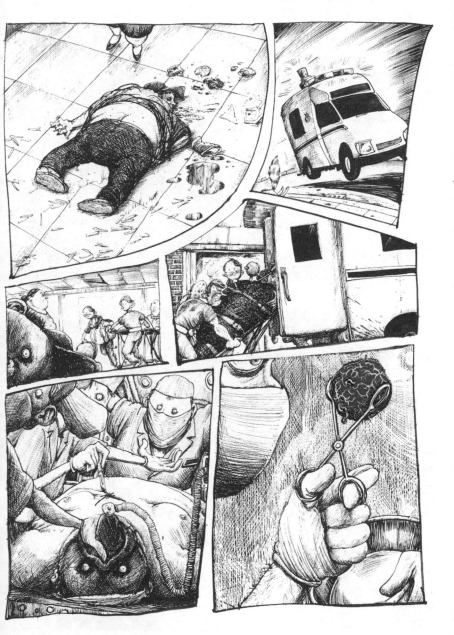

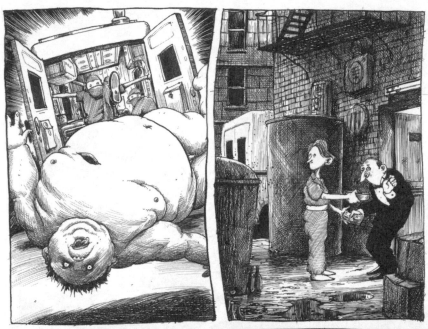

Greed

Dylan Evans

Sin is not what it used to be. Gluttony is now a psychological problem for which we should feel sympathy, rather than a vice that must be condemned. Pride has been renamed 'self-esteem' and is encouraged by a thousand self-help books. And lust is positively *de rigueur*.

Only greed still inspires the same revulsion that it did when Pope Gregory I compiled a list of seven deadly sins some fifteen centuries ago, and public condemnation grew even more florid in the aftermath of the financial crisis of 2008. 'Sick of greedy bankers gambling with your money?' asked the British Co-operative Party on its Facebook page, while the Occupy Wall Street protesters proclaimed themselves to be 'the 99 per cent that will no longer tolerate the greed and corruption of the 1 per cent.'

The apparent continuity should not, however, obscure the radical difference between the Christian and secular censure of greed. In both cases, greed means wanting too much, but the reference point is different. For Christians, greed means wanting more than is consistent with attaining the ultimate goal of life – eternal salvation. Saint Thomas Aquinas wrote that greed was 'a sin against God, just as all mortal sins, in as much as man condemns things eternal for the sake of temporal things.' In 'Purgatory', the second part of Dante's *Divine Comedy*, the penitents were bound and laid face down on the ground for having concentrated too much on earthly thoughts.

This heavenly standard is not, however, what animated the Co-operative Party or the Occupy Wall Street protesters. From a secular perspective, greed means wanting more than your fair share, and a fair share does not necessarily imply complete equality; some degree of inequality is permissible, though exactly how much inequality can be tolerated is a matter for empirical investigation. According to a survey conducted in 2011, Americans think that the ideal income distribution would be for the top quintile to have 30 per cent of the nation's wealth. In reality, the richest fifth of the US population had 85 per cent of the wealth in the same year. So people naturally conclude that the distribution of wealth is unfair, and that those at the top are being greedy.

Behavioural economists have explored our feelings about inequality and greed by means of something called the 'ultimatum game'. In this experimental setup, two strangers are paired and given a sum of money. One of them – usually referred to as the 'proposer' – has to decide how to divvy it up. The proposer might suggest a 50/50 split, or they might drive a hard bargain and offer only 10 per cent to the other person. The other player (usually referred to as the 'responder') can either accept this offer, or reject it. If the responder accepts, each player walks away with the share stipulated by the proposer. If the responder rejects the offer, each player is left with nothing.

According to game theory, a rational proposer should always offer the smallest amount possible, and a rational responder should always accept the proposer's offer, no matter how meagre it is. After all, some money is always better than none. But this isn't what real people actually do when they play this game. Instead of offering the smallest possible amount, most proposers offer between 40 and 50 per cent, and on the few occasions that proposers offer less than 20 per cent, responders reject about half of those offers. In other words, responders prefer to punish greedy proposers and walk away with nothing rather than accept a derisory offer. Anticipating that reaction, most proposers curb their greed.

These findings have been replicated many times in studies all around the world, which strongly suggests that most people care about other things in addition to their own personal gains and losses – things like fairness and equality.

Interestingly, the only groups that do not fit this pattern are those that exhibit a low degree of market integration, an index devised by anthropologists that combines the existence of a labour market for cash wages, the farming of crops for cash, and the existence of a national language (rather than a local dialect). In cultures with the least amount of market integration, people behave almost as greedily as game theory suggests they should when playing the ultimatum game. Machiguenga farmers in Peru, for example, offer much less than usual, and accept almost every offer.

This runs counter to a common view about capitalism in which market economies and greed are often thought to go hand in hand. Speaking on the BBC in June 2012, the economist Lord Robert Skidelsky confidently asserted that 'capitalist civilization has unleashed greed from its traditional moral constraint'. The cross-cultural comparisons of behaviour in the ultimatum game suggest, though, that the exact opposite may be true, and that far from unleashing greed, the growth of trade and markets would seem to promote the spread of sharing norms and ideas about what constitutes fair exchange.

Sharing norms are a cultural invention, not an innate part of human nature. Hunter-gatherers share meat in a variety of ways, but none of them is a model of courtesy. In one system, known as 'tolerated theft', empty-handed people steal morsels from a successful hunter in the knowledge that he will be too lazy to stop them. In 'demand sharing', everyone begs the person with the meat to give them a bit, and in the general cacophony that results, the loudest voice wins. Nothing could be further from the 'primitive communism' envisaged by Marx, in which noble savages distributed the spoils of the hunt to each according to his need. On the contrary, in real foraging societies, meat is distributed to each according to his greed.

It is likely that sharing norms only began to evolve with the development of long-range trading between unrelated groups. In the Mediterranean region this seems to have begun around 35,000 BC, as trade routes sprang up along the Danube. From there it was a long, slow journey to the merchant bankers who financed grain trading in medieval Italy, and on to the complex mechanisms of today's global economy. The gradual development of market mechanisms, in other words, would have been impossible without the coevolution of norms about what constitutes a disinterested and just exchange. Paradoxically, then, the accusations of greed and unfairness that are levelled at capitalism today have only been made possible by the growth of capitalism itself. Capitalism may lead to greater social inequality, but it also gives people the tools to denounce inequality and impose constraints on greed.

For some critics, the connection between capitalism and greed is deeper than merely one of imposing or removing constraints. Greed, they argue, plays a crucial role in the very foundations of capitalism. The most famous of these critics is, of course, Karl Marx, who decried 'the intrinsic connection between private property, greed, the alienation of labour, capital and landed property', and the defenders of capitalism's response has tended to be that greed is simply part of human nature – that Marxists are living in a fantasy world if they believe they can dislodge it. According to neoclassical economics, the fundamental problem facing any economy is that resources are limited but human needs and wants are infinite. There is, in other words, no natural satiation point; no point at which *Homo economicus* can say, 'I have enough of everything I want'.

Some anthropologists disagree, arguing that infinite wants are a historical development, a product of capitalism itself rather than an eternal part of what we call 'human nature'. The anthropologist Marshall Sahlins famously argued that 'the present human condition of man slaving to bridge the gap between his unlimited wants and his insufficient means is a tragedy of modern times', and contrasted this with the situation of our hunter-gatherer ancestors, 'in which all the people's material wants were easily satisfied'.

> There are two possible courses to affluence. Wants may be 'easily satisfied' either by producing much or desiring little. The familiar conception, the Galbraithean way – based on the concept of market economies – states that man's wants are great, not to say infinite, whereas his means are limited, although they can be improved. Thus, the gap between means and ends can be narrowed by industrial productivity, at least to the point that 'urgent goods' become plentiful. But there is also a Zen road to affluence, which states that human material wants are finite and few, and technical means unchanging but on the whole adequate. Adopting the Zen strategy, a people can enjoy an unparalleled material plenty – with a low standard of living. That, I think, describes the hunters.

This romantic view of hunter-gatherers as noble savages uncorrupted by capitalist greed echoes older colonial accounts, such as that of Paul Le Jeune, a Jesuit missionary in French Canada who, in 1634, wrote that 'our Savages are happy; for the two tyrants who provide hell and torture for many of our Europeans, do not reign in their great forests – I mean ambition and avarice as they are contented with a mere living, not one of them gives himself to the Devil to acquire wealth.'

Yet there is reason to be skeptical of these rosy pictures. The egalitarianism of hunter-gatherer societies is due not to the absence of greed, but to the peculiar constraints imposed by the hunter-gatherer mode of existence. The nomadic nature of that existence means that people must carry all they possess, and so only possess what they can carry. It was not until our ancestors first started farming, around 10,000 years ago, and made the transition from nomadism to a sedentary existence, that this constraint disappeared and the process of accumulating wealth could begin.

What this goes to show is that greed is not a cultural invention (a novelty grafted on to our psyche by the introduction of farming, or capitalism, or any other historical development) but rather an innately specified element of being human that developed through natural selection. Our chances of surviving and reproducing depend crucially on access to a wide range of resources and if there were any prehistoric humans without acquisitive tendencies, their non-acquisitive genes appear to have died with them.

This is not to say that humans are thoroughly selfish. Examples of altruistic decency abound, but evolutionary biologists have long recognized that altruism can only evolve under very special conditions, and even then it is predicated on the basis of a fundamental underlying selfishness. To take one example, a mother may be spectacularly generous when caring for her own children, but mundanely selfish when confronted with another woman's brood.

The fact that greed is natural does not imply, of course, that 'greed is good', to quote Oliver Stone's Gordon Gekko. To assume that it did would be to commit the naturalistic fallacy. Debates about the morality or immorality of greed cannot be resolved by appealing solely to empirical evidence about its origins or ubiquity. Disease is natural and yet we strive to overcome it. Likewise, someone may accept that greed is part of human nature and yet condemn it as a vice.

It's worth quoting Gekko's infamous speech in detail:

> Greed, for lack of a better word, is good. Greed is right. Greed works. Greed clarifies, cuts through, and captures, the essence of the evolutionary spirit. Greed, in all of its forms; greed for life, for money, for love, knowledge,

has marked the upward surge of mankind and greed, you mark my words, will not only save Teldar Paper, but that other malfunctioning corporation called the USA.

These words derive their dramatic impact, of course, from the contrast with the common assumption that greed is bad, and most viewers probably took them as yet more evidence of Gekko's unscrupulous character, rather than as an invitation to re-examine that common assumption. But this just goes to show how entrenched the assumption is. Let us not be so quick. Let us pause for a moment and ask ourselves what it is about greed that so many people find distasteful.

A clue lies in the professions of those who are typically accused of greed. Footballers and pop stars may earn as much or more than bankers and CEOs, and yet the former are rarely criticized for being greedy. Clearly, it is not income inequality per se that irks, but something to do with finance (and finance as a vocation) more generally.

This prejudice has a long pedigree. Moneylenders have been persecuted throughout history and this persecution has often been tinged with elements of racism and xenophobia. In medieval Europe, lending money was one of the few occupations permitted to Jews, and when it made them rich they were further tyrannized, not only because they were not Christians, but also because killing them was a quick way to expunge debts. The figure of the evil Jewish speculator is still a powerful cultural icon. Only a decade ago Malaysia's Prime Minister Mahathir Mohamad blamed his country's problems on the machinations of Jewish speculators. A survey in the *Boston Review* in 2009 found that 25 per cent of non-Jewish Americans blamed Jews for the financial crisis, with a higher percentage among Democrats than Republicans.

This is not to say that the current obsession with 'greedy bankers' is simply a disguised form of anti-Semitism, but it does suggest that the condemnation of a particular form of greed is merely the visible tip of an iceberg whose submerged base consists of a complex (and often confused) set of atavistic prejudices, economic theories and political beliefs. And even if we restrict ourselves to the economic and political aspects of this iceberg, it may be hard to dissect the many implicit notions that lurk beneath the surface of consciousness. But many of these notions seem to involve unexamined assumptions about fairness, justice, equality, private property and public goods, which together constitute a loose definition of what we think of as socialism.

So perhaps accusations of greed are merely a smoke screen for pushing a socialist agenda? A Trojan Horse by means of which socialist assumptions are smuggled in to the debate under the guise of taking the moral high ground? This would certainly be consistent with the more general distinction between the ways that socialists and capitalists tend to portray each other, with capitalists regarding socialists as misinformed and naïve and socialists perceiving capitalists as downright evil.

In keeping with traditional modes of Christian thinking about greed, modern secular judgements imply that it is not just bad for society, but also bad for the greedy person himself. From a Christian perspective, greed is bad because it can lead to eternal damnation, but from a secular point of view the harmful effects of greed are dissatisfaction and unhappiness.

Take the story of King Midas, for example. The fabled king's greed makes him miserable; his initial joy at his new-found power to turn everything to gold is soon replaced by disappointment and regret when he realizes that he can't eat anything. But of course we should be careful what moral we infer from this story; surely the source of the king's misfortune is not greed but stupidity, and if greed is to blame for anything here, it is that it so overwhelmed the king's mind that no room for forethought was left, in which case, greed is not bad in itself, but merely poses a danger for rational decision-making. Providing, then, that greed is exercised in an intelligent fashion, it should not lead to any deleterious consequences for the greedy person.

But it is precisely the possibility of intelligent greed that the skeptics doubt, and they can point to evidence from neuroscience to support their concerns. According to the psychologist Ian Robertson, 'power and money both act on the brain's reward system, which, if over-stimulated for long periods, develops appetites that are difficult to satisfy, just as is the case for drug addiction. We call these appetites greed and greedy people are never satisfied.'

The comparison with drug addiction is instructive, for it is a paradigmatic example of how an uncontrollable desire for something can crowd out rational deliberation. The desire for greater wealth can, Robertson claims, become similarly uncontrollable, but then the problem is not greed itself; it is, rather, *uncontrollable* greed, just as the problem with drug addiction is not the desire for drugs, but the uncontrollable desire for them. The number of drug addicts is minuscule compared to the number of people who regularly consume drugs in a responsible manner and are able to control these appetites. In the same way, those who cannot master their desire for riches are no doubt vastly outnumbered by those who can.

Rather less dramatic is the ubiquitous metaphor of the hedonic treadmill, which describes greed as something that can never lead to true satisfaction because the goal of attaining greater wealth is a moving target. We adapt rather too quickly to increased fortune. The pleasure of becoming a millionaire, for instance, soon fades, and before long one desires to become a multimillionaire. The quest for riches is therefore like running on a treadmill, where, to cite the Red Queen, 'it takes all the running you can do, to keep in the same place'.

The treadmill effect arises from two mechanisms, one psychological and the other social. The psychological mechanism is habituation, whereby we get used to good fortune, so that a sudden increase in our wealth feels wonderful at first but soon comes to feel normal and unremarkable. The social mechanism is 'keeping up with the Joneses'; if my new car gives me satisfaction because it is flashier than my neighbour's, then it also no doubt makes my neighbor envious, and before long he too will buy a car that is just as eye-catching (or even more so) and my brief moment of pride is over.

The economist Robert Frank has argued that while the social treadmill may leave us all in the same place relative to each other, it makes us all worse off in some absolute sense, because keeping up with the Joneses carries implications that often escape our attention. In order to buy that flashy car (a 'positional' good), we may have to work longer hours and spend less time with our friends and family (i.e. give up 'non-positional' goods, or goods whose value does not depend on the opinions of others).

Both kinds of treadmill are intended to illustrate the self-defeating nature of greed, but these arguments only apply if one prefers laziness to exercise, and there are many people who enjoy running on treadmills. We cannot rule out the possibility, therefore, that for some people the pursuit of wealth may be its own reward. With the psychological treadmill, it may be that the idea of setting goals, achieving them, and then setting new goals, is more appealing to some than an unchanging state of bliss. Similarly, in the case of the social treadmill it may be the very process of competition, rather than the outcome, that motivates some. Also, Frank's argument also neglects the very real possibility that we *don't* all end up with the same relative positions. Unless social mobility is zero, some will end up better off than others because not all the neighbours will be *able* to keep up and those who have more will therefore be happier, since, as Frank admits, satisfaction depends heavily on one's relative position. As the late Gore Vidal famously quipped: 'It is not enough to succeed. Others must fail.'

Indeed, there is likely to be substantial individual variation with respect to greed, just as there is with most psychological traits. Some people want more than others. Is this a defect in those who want more, or in those who want less? Or should we just accept that this is just a matter of taste, and refrain from criticizing anyone for being too greedy, or too ascetic?

Those with no taste for riches may be incapable of tolerating their greedy brethren, and if the dislike of greed is too entrenched in their minds, they may persist in seeing it as symptomatic of some woeful inner lack, rather than as a healthy motivator. But in that case, those of us who are naturally greedy might go on the offensive too. If the temperate insist on portraying their own frugality as morally superior, rather than merely a difference of taste, then the greedy may insist on pointing out the self-serving nature of their moralizing, for it has always been tempting to detect a whiff of sour grapes in those who condemn greed.

In his most notorious work on ethics, *On the Genealogy of Morality* (1887), Friedrich Nietzsche famously dissects the process by which those with less try to make themselves feel better about the situation they are in by creating an alternative morality for themselves. He claims that there were originally two kinds of people – 'the noble, the powerful, the superior, and the high-minded' and the 'low, low-minded, and plebeian'. At first, goodness was associated with those who were superior, noble and privileged, but the descendants of the lower class came to resent being so powerless, and engineered a 'radical transvaluation of all values' in which the meanings of 'good' and 'bad' were reversed. It is this alternative moral system, according to which the powerless are good and the powerful are bad, that Nietzsche famously calls the 'slave morality'.

Nietzsche argues that the slave morality is ultimately based on bad faith, or a refusal on the part of the 'plebs' to acknowledge that they also used to hunger after wealth and power. Rather than admitting that they have failed to achieve their desires, and trying harder, they pretend that they never wanted to be rich in the first place, and elevate their failure into a virtue.

Nietzsche's arguments may strike the modern ear as presenting too dichotomous a view of humanity, but the rhetoric of 'the 99 per cent that will no longer tolerate the greed and corruption of the 1 per cent' is just as dichotomous, which suggests that there is little chance that either side will succeed in persuading the other to adopt its point of view. Yet, while adherents of the slave morality may never come to see greed as good in itself, they may be persuaded that it has what economists like to call 'positive network externalities'. In other words, greed can be good for society. Indeed, some social institutions, such as free markets, actually *require* individual greed in order to work at all. As Adam Smith famously put it in *The Wealth of Nations*:

> It is not from the benevolence of the butcher, the brewer, or the baker, that we expect our dinner, but from their regard to their own interest. We

address ourselves, not to their humanity but to their self-love, and never talk to them of our own necessities but of their advantages. Nobody but a beggar chooses to depend chiefly upon the benevolence of his fellow citizens.

Building on Smith's analysis, the historian Niall Ferguson argued in his 2012 Reith Lectures that 'it was not biblical virtue that made eighteenth-century England richer than almost anywhere in the world, but rather secular vices.' Even the financial speculators that are so often demonized play a vital role in a market economy. As Victor Niederhoffer, an American-hedge fund manager, explains:

When a harvest is too small to satisfy consumption at its normal rate, speculators come in, hoping to profit from the scarcity by buying. Their purchases raise the price, thereby checking consumption so that the smaller supply will last longer. Producers encouraged by the high price further lessen the shortage by growing or importing to reduce the shortage. On the other side, when the price is higher than the speculators think the facts warrant, they sell. This reduces prices, encouraging consumption and exports and helping to reduce the surplus.

In other words, in their search for profits, speculators send signals to producers and consumers which convey useful information about levels of supply and demand.

To illustrate his point, Niederhoffer refers to the Siege of Antwerp by the Spanish in 1584–1585. In response to the blockade, nearby farmers grew more grain, which was smuggled into Antwerp at great peril. Speculators, guessing that bread was going to be scarce, pushed up prices through shrewd purchases, and the bakers responded by baking even more.

But the Antwerp politicians disapproved of the greedy speculators profiting from war. They set a very low ceiling on the price of bread, and prescribed severe penalties for violators. The result? Bakers could no longer afford to pay the smugglers, who stopped running the blockades, and the supply of grain dried up. The Antwerpers surrendered and the city was annexed by Spain.

But what about the supposed role of greed in causing the financial crisis of 2008? Even if we concede that greed can have positive externalities in the right conditions, surely, the critics argue, there are times when greed is so excessive that it is downright dangerous?

Yet even this is not clear. There is something deeply regressive about blaming the financial crisis on individual psychology. One of the greatest breakthroughs of the

Enlightenment was the recognition that social progress could be advanced more effectively by building good institutions than by attempting to reform human nature. Thinkers like Adam Smith, Bernard Mandeville, Alexander Hamilton and James Madison argued that societies with the right institutions can flourish even when the individuals who live in them remain as greedy and venal as ever.

These thinkers espoused what the psychologist Steven Pinker has referred to as the Tragic Vision – the view that 'humans are inherently limited in virtue, wisdom, and knowledge and social arrangements must acknowledge those limits'. By implication, it is pointless to blame social ills on moral failings, since these are a given.

Those who blame the financial crisis on greed often ignore these insights and hark back to an earlier time, when reform was a matter for the soul rather than society. In Pinker's terminology, they espouse a Utopian Vision, according to which human failings can ultimately be eliminated. If certain social ills are caused by individual greed, then those ills can only be cured by abolishing greed. But what would a world without greed look like?

For one thing, capitalism could not exist. Without the desire to acquire more than others, there would be no competition, so the only kind of economic system that could survive would be a communist one. Asked what he thought about Marxism, the evolutionary biologist E. O. Wilson quipped: 'Wonderful theory, wrong species.' He meant that communism was more suited to ants than to humans, but if greed was eliminated from human nature we might well become like social insects, living for the collective rather than for our own individual needs and desires. We would lose a sense of the self as an independent entity and our individual identities would be submerged in the hive mind. All forms of individual excellence and self-expression would vanish.

Such extreme collectivism has been a common feature of dystopian science fiction ever since Yevgeny Zamyatin completed his novel *We* in 1921. The protagonist D-503 lives in the One State, where people march in step and wear identical clothing. In Ayn Rand's 1937 novella *Anthem*, Equality 7-2521 tells a tale of complete socialization and governmental control using only plural pronouns, as people are burned at the stake for saying an Unspeakable Word such as I, Me, or Myself. In the 1998 computer-animated film *Antz*, a neurotic worker ant called Z-4195 yearns to break out of the suffocating conformity of his society and express himself.

Like King Midas, those who condemn greed should be careful what they wish for.

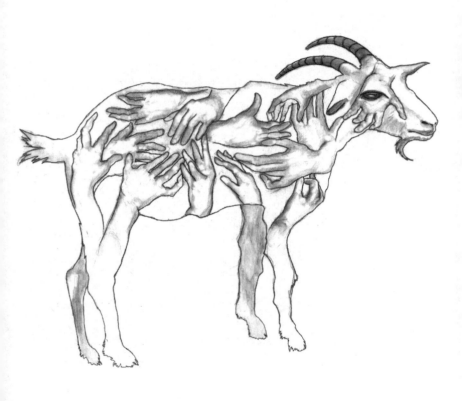

Lust

David Flusfeder

I met NW in New York in the mid-1980s. She was introduced to me by Paul and Sean, who had made friends with her after finding her weeping on West 4th Street.

NW was in her early twenties, a couple of years younger than me. She was quick-witted and funny, as most German women I've met are. She had high cheekbones and short dark brown hair, which she combed sideways, like a pre-war schoolboy. Her features were dainty and pretty and she looked like a slightly stockier version of the actress Isabella Rossellini, whom she was fascinated by to an almost stalkerish extent. Her capacity for neurosis – the public weeping, Isabella Rossellini – only added to her beauty in my eyes and anyway was both understandable and forgivable. Her mother had had a tradition of threatening suicide once a year; on her birthday she would listen to a recording of Mahler's Symphony No. 5 and arrange her suicide paraphernalia around her – the pills, the freshly written note – and then, when the music was over, put it all away for another year. Two years before, she had finally gone through with it. NW's father was an industrialist from Stuttgart who collected memorial jewellery made from dead people's hair.

I didn't know these details about NW yet. She would tell me about them later, after the Florida Shark Show; but I had met her a couple of times with Paul and Sean and fallen for her. Our early relationship, such as it was, was mediated through movie stars. We disagreed on James Dean, but we could agree entirely on Julie Christie or, more precisely, the Julie Christie of 1963. It seemed like a vindication of something that was yet to come that at thirteen we'd both had movie stills of Julie Christie in *Billy Liar* on our bedroom walls.

NW was studying film at NYU. I was working as a proofreader and, in an aimless kind of way, trying to write fiction. Paul was the link between us all: he was a graphic designer at the magazine where I worked and he lived in the same Lower East Side building as Sean, who was a medieval historian.

It was autumn, and the four of us had been at the Museum of Modern Art, where NW and I discovered similar tastes for the work of anyone who went to a great deal of trouble to make something inexplicable, and then we all walked downtown to Little Italy for the Feast of San Genarro.

Every September, to celebrate the patron saint of Naples, Little Italy turns into a mess of food stalls and carnival sideshows and visitors from New Jersey drinking and eating and pretending they're extras in *The Godfather*. By accident, or maybe it was the spirit of Julie Christie that was guiding us, NW and I became separated from the others in the crowd. Somehow a big wheel was squeezed into the alleyway on Mulberry Street behind the Puck Building, and NW and I took a ride on it, bumping against each other, spinning over the fair. And afterwards, still giddy on land, we went into the next sideshow. We dropped our dollar bills into a bucket held by a small bored-looking man, who watched without interest as we struggled through a curtain into a darkened trailer.

We sat down on a cold wooden ramp, facing three wide roller-blinds that were drawn shut. The rest of the audience was made up of four children, one man and a dog. The children were eating potato chips, the man and the dog seemed to be asleep.

Then the music started, loud and military, on crackly tape. A pre-recorded male voice lifted above it.

'Ladies and gentlemen, boys and girls,' it said, 'welcome to the Florida Shark Show, here in Coney

Island for the very first time!'

We weren't in Coney Island, we were on Mulberry Street, but the voice wasn't to know that.

'What you are about to see will astound you!' it promised.

I was prepared to be astounded. My shoulders and NW's brushed together in the dark. The lights flickered on and the bored-looking man ambled across to pull up the blinds and reveal:

'The Largest Moveable Aquarium In The World!' said the voice.

There were three small sleepy sharks inside the grey water. One was comatose on the floor of the tank. A second drifted aimlessly back and forth. The third bumped its snout against the glass, close to where the ladder was.

'Terrifying killer sharks,' said the voice. 'Don't be fooled. They may look small, but the concave glass makes them look smaller than they really are.'

I can speak for NW. Despite the advice, we were fooled: this was one of those moments when two people could be sure, without comment or doubt, that they are having the same experience. Our shoulders stayed pressed together.

'And now, here is The Death-Defying Miss Atlantis entering the tank!'

The words were premature. The action was already lagging behind its description on the tape. Maybe

Miss Atlantis had missed her cue or maybe she was just slower than she used to be. The fat middle-aged lady in a fake leopard-skin bikini with an oxygen tank strapped to her back was still climbing slowly and a little awkwardly into the tank when, according to the tape, she was already swimming inside it.

'These sharks are deadly,' thrilled the tape. 'Knife-sharp teeth inside vice-like jaws – and not just the teeth! How about that skin?! Like hundreds of tiny razor blades, the slightest touch will draw *blood*. And,' the voice gasped, 'we all know what happens when sharks smell BLOOD! Don't we?'

We both laughed. I wanted to kiss her and later I would, but for the moment there seemed something perfect about our shoulder-touch and I didn't want to ruin it. Miss Atlantis swam slowly back and forth to the amazement of the tape. Defying death, she grabbed the fin of the only swimming shark and allowed herself to be towed across the largest moveable aquarium in the world.

'And now!' squealed the voice, as the music rose to a new pitch of violence and drama, 'here is the most dangerous part of the act. Miss Atlantis will have to take her eyes off the sharks in order to climb out of the tank.'

The words were again ahead of the action. Miss Atlantis was submerged, still swimming with the sharks, but the voice pressed on regardless.

'First one hand, then the second, and she pulls and, and, a-a-a-AND OUT SHE GETS! LADIES AND GENTLEMEN, BOYS AND GIRLS, LET'S HEAR IT FOR THE FABULOUS DEATH-DEFYING MISS ATLANTIS AND THE FLORIDA SHARK SHOW HERE IN CONEY ISLAND FOR THE VERY FIRST TIME!'

The children applauded, because they were being told to. The dog stretched out and shook himself. The music was already dying when she finally lifted first one hand and then the second, and finally heaved her body out of the water; but the bottom part of her fake leopard-skin bikini slipped down over her legs and splashed in as The Fabulous Death-Defying Miss Atlantis, showing the pitted cheeks of her arse, climbed out of the tank.

We clapped and we cheered. Miss Atlantis returned, to stand by the exit. She was wrapped in a large blue towel and holding an empty collection bucket. We threw a few dollar bills into the bucket and the bored-looking man came back inside to roll down the blinds and hide the three small drugged sharks from view. We lingered a while, but neither retrieved the leopard-skin bikini-bottom, which continued to float on the surface of the largest moveable aquarium in the world, and we walked out, into what seemed like a different afternoon.

I was falling deeper in love. Being with NW made

me, for the first time in my life, want to write poetry. I still have some of the poems I subsequently wrote. They make me wince to think about them now, with their coy sentiments about the eroticism of the hairs on her arms, but poems demand an honesty upon their writer, which was good training for fiction-writing, and writing them made me realise that a large part of what I was feeling for NW was simple, although complicated, lust.

Lust begins with appetite. There is something proprietorial, even predatory about this, the desire to possess the object, maybe to the point of consuming it – but whereas love can take its object as an abstraction (the lover ignores his loved one's flaws, as he extrapolates from the physical to the ideal), the object of lust is perceived in its full physicality.

Fetishism takes the part instead of the whole: a foot-fetishist celebrates the sole of his mistress's foot; all he needs is the stamp of that foot upon his unprotected body to reach his kind of ecstasy. But I wasn't a fetishist. When I gazed upon the hairs of NW's arms it wasn't because those would suffice. It was because their physical fact excited me (gave me, in Thomas Pynchon's serendipitous phrase, that familiar 'recto-genital throb'), and because the part was an emblem of the whole, the desired body, NW's, that was crossing Houston Street beside mine.

We had lost Sean and Paul and neither of us seemed

to mind. We were still in that mood that had been created at the Florida Shark Show. We stopped for a drink and some food at a café on Lafayette Street, where I talked a little about my parents, and she told me about hers. And we talked about happiness, which, she said, was an impossible thing, at least for her.

I knew that she was half in love with me, or at least with an idea that she could fit a notion of me inside. I was English (or English-ish), which was useful for any number of movie-derived fantasies that we could play out together. Crossing the Bowery against the traffic, she could imagine the two of us driving around black-and-white English countryside in James Dean's car; I was Cary Grant, she was Isabella Rossellini. We would stop off in picturesque fields. I, with my Archibald Leach circus training, could leap nimbly out of the car, open the passenger door, lead her into a barn or a field, where I would push her into the long grass, and then...? And then, her imagination stopped, because NW was a lesbian.

NW had made no secret of being a lesbian. This complicated matters, a further impediment between desire and its consummation, and my heterosexuality made me feel somehow brutish next to her, as if to be a lesbian was to have reached a more evolved state.

I wanted to kiss her, and later I would, but for the moment I was too shy to attempt it. I wished that I were bolder but I didn't know quite how to negotiate a path through this. Part of my timidity, I think, was an anxiety of what might happen afterwards, if she accepted my kiss; but the greater part of course was the expectation of being rebuffed, because lust is worth nothing unless it's reciprocated.

Lust, Sean had told me, one congenial afternoon a week or two before he and Paul had introduced me to NW, was condemned in the Christian Middle Ages even in marriage. Good Christians were meant to practise an attitude of *contemptus mundi* (that is, 'contempt for the world'); and any of the exigencies or urgencies of the body – or indeed anything that appealed to the senses – were manifestations of base matter, the Fall.

Sean was not a religious man, but on the walls of his studio were postcards of carved figures from Amiens Cathedral. Most of them were kissing, grappling, embracing. He explained to me that these had been designed not as incitements to lust but as warning reminders of the sin.

Lust, or *luxuria* as it was known in the clerical texts, was seen as an overspilling of animalistic urges when the individual was meant to be rising above his or her base origins to contemplate and move closer towards the divine. Surrounding the window that opened onto Sean's fire escape were illustrations of lust's consequences: one woman had her breasts bitten by a dragon; another was suckling a pair of toads; a third's nude body was enwrapped by the coils of a serpent while blood dripped from her mouth.

This aspect of Christianity had been there from the beginning. The gospel of Matthew quotes Jesus as saying:

> But I say to you that whoever looks at a woman to lust for her has already committed adultery with her in his heart. If your right eye causes you to sin, pluck it out and cast it from you; for it is more profitable for you that one of your members perish, than for your whole body to be cast into hell. And if your right hand causes you to sin, cut it off and cast it from you; for it is more profitable for you that one of your members perish, than for your whole body to be cast into hell.

The Church Fathers followed this. Michel Foucault, in *The History of Sexuality*, writes of St Augustine's 'rather horrifying description of the sex act... as a kind of spasm'. Augustine says, 'This sexual act takes such a complete and passionate possession of the whole man, both physically and emotionally, that what results is the keenest of all pleasures on the level of sensations, and at the crisis of excitement it practically paralyses all power of deliberate thought.'

I couldn't quite see the problem in this, but Sean wasn't ready to argue the Augustinian position and neither was he going to tell me more about the history of lust, clerical or otherwise, because all he really wanted that afternoon was for me to hear about his unrequited desire for Paul, who gave of himself freely, except to Sean, because, Paul told him, he didn't want to spoil their friendship ('I don't give a fuck about friendship!' Sean said); so most of what follows here I've had to learn for myself, based on some of the clues he gave me.

Part of the problem for Augustine was the penis's rebellious behaviour, a revolt against man and God (the reason Adam covered his genitals was not shame at his nakedness but embarrassment at the movements of his wayward penis):

> Sometimes this lust importunes them in spite of themselves, and sometimes fails them when they desire to feel it, so that though lust rages in the mind, it stirs not in the body. Thus, strangely enough, this emotion not only fails to obey the legitimate desire to beget offspring, but also refuses to serve lascivious lust; and though it often opposes its whole combined energy to the soul that resists it, sometimes also it is divided against itself, and while it moves the soul, leaves the body unmoved.

Martin Luther had a more pragmatic view: 'Nature never lets up. We are all driven to the secret sin. To say it crudely but honestly, if it doesn't go into a woman, it goes into your shirt.' But he kept to the Augustinian view of the sex act itself: 'so hideous and frightful that physicians compare it with epilepsy or falling sickness'. And it's not just Christianity. The Hindu *Bhagavad Gita* has Krishna warn that lust is one of the gates to hell. Sikhs count lust among the Five Cardinal Sins. The third Precept of Theravada Buddhism is to 'refrain from unchastity'. (Other groups of Buddhists may not be so proscriptive, but all acknowledge the dangers of lust as a debilitating form of attachment.) A Taoist saying has it that 'Anyone who commits debauchery and indulges in sex will suffer from insanity. Having passed through this, he will be born among the sows and the boars.'

Judaism and Islam are less prudish. They do warn their adherents against the corrupting properties of lust and sexual incontinence, but Judaism has the notion of *yetzer* – sexual desire as a necessary force in the universe that can lead to either good or evil – which is similar to the Islamic image of the two opposed natures in man. The issue is balance. Judaism and Islam are quite a long way away from traditional Christianity here. Actually, they're closer to Mayan thought than Christian. Tlazolteotl, the 'Filth Goddess' of the Maya, was the patroness of adulterous and promiscuous women, who engendered pollution and then swept it away with her broom.

This is how the ancient Greeks saw it too: their gods had robust sexual lives, both with other gods and with mortals. Greek religious rites used sexual language, images and behaviour to appeal to the divine good will. It was when sexual desire became less restrained (as in Plato's pre-Islamic metaphor in *Phaedrus* of the horse of desire, which, if uncontrolled by its twin of reason, will pull the soul's chariot to ruin) that it could pollute temples and bring disaster on the city. As the statesman and rhetorician Aeschines said 'unrestrained physical pleasures and a feeling that nothing is ever enough, these are what recruit to gangs of robbers, what fill the pirate ships, these are each man's Fury; these are what drive him to slaughter his fellow citizens, serve tyrants, conspire to overthrow democracy.'

Similarly, the Romans of the republic did not see sexual desire or activity as unclean unless it overspilled acceptable boundaries, as when prostitutes entered the temple, or vestal virgins took lovers, or a citizen allowed himself to be sexually penetrated.

Despite *luxuria* being a carnal sin, lust is there in the Christian religious texts, all the same. The carnal fervour of The Song of Songs is unmistakeable, which the Christian tradition has piously, and somewhat implausibly, recast as a metaphor for devotion to God

('Let him kiss me with the kiss of his mouth: for thy breasts are better than wine'). Sean did point out, in between complaints about Paul's casual cruelty ('Why not me?!'), that you have to look at the historical context: the Jewish origins, in the wandering tribe of Israelites, demand fertility; Christianity, unlike Judaism, is a religion of End Times; you don't need to exhort the tribe to procreate when the Last Judgement is at hand. (St Paul: 'The body is not for fornication, but for the Lord: and the Lord for the body.')

The Christians, as in their gloss on The Song of Songs, couldn't help eroticising the divine, and this is heard clearly in the language of the mystics: Mechthild of Magdeburg spoke of how 'the most Beloved goes toward the Most Beautiful in the hidden chambers of the invisible deity' where God promises to satisfy eternally 'your noble desire and your insatiable hunger'. And Bernard of Clairvaux, the great enemy of Peter Abelard, wrote:

> It is my belief that to a person so disposed, God will not refuse that most intimate kiss of all, a mystery of supreme generosity and ineffable sweetness … And finally, when we shall have obtained these favours through many prayers and tears, we humbly dare to raise our eyes to his mouth, so divinely beautiful, not merely to gaze

upon it, but I say it with fear and trembling – to receive its kiss.

Following the influence of St Francis, some of the sicklier death-cult aspects of Christianity were ameliorated. When he wasn't pining for Paul, Sean might sometimes be persuaded to recite medieval love lyrics that could be quite wanton and pagan-sounding or the less interesting courtly stuff of the troubadors, who sang of the greatest love that would be unconsummated except by a kiss. Which, I feared, was what was happening with me and NW. The suitor gains a kiss, but if he wins more, then love itself will die. As Andreas Capellanus put it:

But I am greatly surprised that you wish to misapply the term 'love' to that marital affection which husband and wife are expected to feel for each other after marriage, since everybody knows that love can have no place between husband and wife. They may be bound to each other by a great and immoderate affection, but their feeling cannot take the place of love, because it cannot fit under the true definition of love. For what is love but an inordinate desire to receive passionately a furtive and hidden embrace? But what embrace between husband and wife can be furtive, I ask you … From this you may see

> clearly that love cannot possibly flourish between you and your husband. Therefore, since every woman of character ought to love, prudently, you can without doing yourself any harm accept the prayers of a suppliant and endow your suitor with your love.

I did not want to marry NW. And I'm sure that Sean didn't want to marry Paul. Both of us knew, I think, that our love was more or less hopeless, but lust does not know reason or sense, or permit much self-consciousness.

Sean did take me through an etymology of lust. The root of the English word is from the Latin 'lustrum', which is actually a period of time, but denotes a purification rite. The word Augustine used that has been translated as 'lust' is *libido*, which means 'desire'. Similarly, when St Paul in the book of Romans preaches to 'make not provision for the flesh, to fulfil the lusts thereof', that's a seventeenth-century gloss on 'desires of the flesh'. And Dante's lovers have committed sins of 'appetite' and 'desire'. The French use the word *luxure* if they're talking about the sin that we call lust; but *luxure* is only used in that religious-historical context, it doesn't overspill into everyday descriptions of behaviour and thought.

On the outer, second ring of Dante's *Inferno*, Dante has his lovers ('they who make reason subject to desire') lashed and buffeted by storms, just as their sin had deranged their senses in life. But not all of them are on their own: lovers who died together are still together. In Dante's topography of hell, at least those convicted of lust are seen as committing a crime of mutuality.

Lust is sexual desire with a bad press agent. The Christian tradition has castigated desire, blaming a failure in morals on the lack of restraint of something that should be, following St Paul, eliminated.

In the seventeenth and eighteenth centuries we can find remarks on lust, and sex, and pleasure, that might have shocked some contemporary readers but sound to us as sympathetically modern. Laclos in *Les Liaisons Dangereuses*, wrote about prudes: 'At the very heart of rapture they remain aloof, offering you only half-delights. That absolute self-abandon, that ecstasy of the senses when pleasure is purified in its own excess, all that is best in love is quite unknown to them.'

This is an echo of something Thomas Hobbes had written a century before. Lust is 'a sensual pleasure, but not only that; there is in it also a delight of the mind: for it consisteth of two appetites together, to please, and to be pleased.'

And this is what lust needs. The Marquis de Sade was sent to the Bastille for the crime of poisoning a prostitute with the aphrodisiac Spanish Fly. Even the most rigorously theoretical of voluptuaries wants what he is feeling to be mutual.

In Plato's *Symposium*, Aristophanes tells of Zeus's affront at the arrogance of the original humans. These were four-legged creatures (some male, with two penises; some hermaphrodite, with a penis and vagina; others female, with two vaginas) that could run so fast they tried to 'scale the heights of heaven and set upon the gods'. In his anger, Zeus cut them all in half. Now humankind is a rabble of lost halves in pursuit of the whole, yearning to combine.

It is difficult enough, especially when young, for a man to comprehend the shape and movements of female desire: even more so if, following Plato's metaphor, the woman comes from a different original. This might be why lesbian sex has become such a staple of male heterosexual pornography. We are not implicated; we can be stimulated by their pleasure because we will never be responsible for it.

Finally we kissed in the back of a cab going back to her apartment. It was quite a chaste kiss but it was a kiss all the same and I hoped it promised more. We had an arrangement to meet Paul and Sean at a bar in the East Village but she seemed reluctant to go.

'Let's do something else,' she said.

I don't know why I argued with her, I don't know why I mulishly insisted we should keep to the plan. I had promised to try to intercede with Paul on Sean's behalf, but I don't think it was because of that. Maybe I was nervous of her, maybe I felt we had been together too long that day and it would spoil unless others were now involved. As long as we had the Florida Shark Show in front of us, or a version of it, nothing could go wrong. Dutifully, I said that we had to keep to the arrangement. She said that she would meet me there. The second kiss we shared was even more chaste than the first.

It was the night of the week when the Boy Bar, on 8th Street, became the Girl Bar. On the downstairs stage, a transvestite was lip-synching to 1970s disco. I was sitting in the upstairs bar with Paul; Sean was on the other side of the room watching us, and Paul and I were getting drunk. He was on vodka, I was on whiskey, and he was telling me stories from his past.

'I'm the way I am because my mother used to beat me naked in the attic,' he said. 'We're Catholics, dumb fucking blue-collar Polish Catholics, and whenever I did anything wrong, she'd take me up to the attic and beat me. That's what made me the way I am.'

'What are you?' I said.

'I'll let you find out,' he said.

We were leaning back against the wall with the front legs of our chairs off the ground. I could recognise the symptoms of lust, as it were, and flattering as it was to be the object of them, I was preoccupied with other things. There was a broken chain of desire in the upstairs room of the Boy Bar that night. Two girls in denim were playing pool in the centre of the room. On the other side, Sean was now talking to our friend Eliza. Sean was lusting after Paul. Paul was lusting after me, and I was lusting after NW, who had just come up the stairs. And the way she was looking at Eliza, it was clear that not only was she choosing to look at her over me, she probably hadn't even noticed yet that I was in the room.

'She's *gorgeous*,' Paul said.

I didn't know whether he was referring to NW or Eliza, either would have been accurate, and I can't remember what I said in return. But I remember watching and continuing to watch as Paul and I grew drunker and Eliza preened under NW's gaze, and Sean was watching Paul and I was watching NW and Paul was talking to me about writing and writers. I think he wanted, among other things, to steer me along a more kindly path than he saw me as taking.

'Have you read Sherwood Anderson? He's really good,' he said, and he almost cried when he talked about Sherwood Anderson. I promised I would read Sherwood Anderson (and I bought a copy of Sherwood Anderson's *Winesburg, Ohio* shortly afterwards, but I still haven't read it; and maybe I should have, maybe that would have steered me along a more kindly path.)

'Michel Foucault,' Paul said. 'Have you ever read Foucault?'

I told him yes, I had read a few things by Foucault. *Discipline and Punish*, *Madness and Civilization*. And then there was *The History of Sexuality*, which he hadn't finished at the time of his death. I asked Paul the same question.

'Have you ever read Foucault?' I said, and Paul laughed.

'I was fucked by Foucault,' he said.

I asked him if it was nice, which was a fatuous thing to say, but Paul didn't seem to mind.

'He's not really my type. I prefer Budweiser truck drivers, but yes, it was nice. He gave me a baby photo to remember him by.'

I do not want to get into the sexual psychologising of famous men, but it seems inescapable to find some meaning in the gift of a baby photo to a passing lover. Paul met Foucault in a bathhouse. Paul had escaped from his blue-collar attic-beating Polish Catholics and was living for a while in San Francisco. Foucault was a visiting professor at the University of Berkeley. I imagine that the photo he gave Paul was one of a stock of many – a courteous gesture, almost a romantic one. But, as Foucault, always alert to nuance, must have known, it contains its own contradictions. Babies are cherishable because of the infinite possibility they seem to promise. Nothing yet has been ruled out. And while it's probably wrong to claim that a baby is entirely a pre-sexual being, it's certainly not aware of any mutuality of experience, or, indeed, of the inner lives, or needs, of others. It is on its own. Not only, in the customarily anonymous world of the pre-AIDS bathhouse, had a French philosopher authored the experience or, at least, signed it, with the gift of a photograph of himself as a baby, he was also in the habit of (I think it's fair to extrapolate this) presenting his lovers, after their act of lust, with a souvenir that referred back to an entirely different category of being.

As I write this, I have a photograph of NW above my desk. It was one she gave me as a keepsake. It was taken, I think in 1984, of two young women standing in front of the artfully graffitied wall of a nightclub. The woman on the right, who is partly cropped out of the frame, has a short quiff, wears a checkered rockabilly jacket, and is gazing at NW in the centre of the picture with a look of admiration, mingled with a kind of amused wariness. NW, in two-thirds profile, is looking past her admirer towards something or someone out of the frame. Her hair is slicked and combed back (not at all the side-parting of memory). She's wearing a loose jacket over a sweater and T-shirt. And she's even more beautiful than I had remembered. Her eyebrows are arched and long, her mouth is partly open, and the expression in her slightly dazed eyes is unmistakeably of sexual appetite; but mixed in with the pleasure of anticipation is the simple pleasure of being. And this is the meaning of it all. The point of lust is not its consummation. After all, the voluptuaries of the Hellfire Club had a sign on their abbey wall in Latin to the effect that the only animals who feel no melancholy after sex are monks and cockerels. (As Shakespeare wrote: 'A bliss in proof, and proved, a very woe.') The point is that it is in the moment of desiring another that we feel most alive, and most ourselves.

Paul had left the Boy Bar with Sean after he was finally convinced that I wasn't going to pretend to be a Budweiser truck driver for him. Eliza had gone home by herself, as had I after a sort of fractured conversation with NW. The possibility had gone even though, for some time after, we persisted with the flirtation and the invention of make-believe plans.

The last time I saw her before moving back to London, we went to a fortune-teller. We'd been walking along together in an aimless way, as if we were nostalgic for something that had never been allowed to happen, and in a sort of shrugging impulse went into a tarot-reader's storefront. The fortune-teller laid out my cards and promised me that I would get married to an Italian woman and have five children and move to Florida. When it was her turn, NW asked if she was ever going to be happy. The fortune-teller, unnecessarily meanly, I thought, told her that her way was going to be a difficult one, but she would at least become rich.

After I returned to London we wrote letters to each other. She sent me a mix tape of Elvis with 'Baby, Let's Play House'; I brutally sent her a photograph of James Dean's Porsche after the car crash, which I photocopied from Kenneth Anger's *Hollywood Babylon*. I can't remember my motivation for that. I think I might have wanted to make her cry. In Dante's hell, at least the sinfully lusting lovers are together. Unrequited lust is an even stronger emotion than unrequited love. Lust needs the possibility of its consummation if it's not to turn ugly.

She came to see me once in London – or, more probably, she happened to be visiting London and came to see me, which isn't quite the same thing. I took her to the Fountain room at Fortnum & Mason because I thought it would amuse her and she complained it was the sort of place her grandmother took her to. That was more or less the end of things. I had already met my (non-Italian) future wife by then. NW went back to New York and occasionally I would hear news of her, and I'm still friends with Sean, who continues to live, with his partner, in the same building as Paul on Clinton Street. I don't know if NW is rich. The last I heard of her was that despite the prophecies, both the fortune-teller's and her own, she was very happy, living with a firewoman in southern California.

Young versus Old

Nicola Barker

STOP! WAIT! DON'T BLINK/FROWN/
GRIMACE/WINCE/AUTOMATICALLY TRASH
THIS MESSAGE!!! The document you are *young*
currently scanning has been sent to your terminal because
of a <u>marked absence</u> in your Public Information Exchange
Records of a perceptible [**Alternative Word Option:
obvious**] interest in: Gene Therapy, Laser Surgery, Youth
Meds and a myriad [**Alternative Word Option: lot**] of
other subjects relating to these special life-style clusters.
RELAX! Your unconscious remains in*v*iolate. We do
not have access to your current Public Information
Exchange Records, merely to the *old* trends, colours
and impulses in your Public Information Exchange
Records.

NOTHING – I REPEAT – NOTHING OF A

LEGALLY INCRIMINATING [**Alternative Word Option: bad**] NATURE lies within this document. This document will not hector [**Alternative Word Option: preach**] or lecture you. You remain *young*, free to *v*oid it at any time and no evidence of it will remain on your *old* memory files. This document upholds your fundamental Human Rights to FOLLOW YOUR DREAMS; to CHOICE; to INFORMATION. This document accepts – WITHOUT RESERVATION – that the aforementioned are crucial [**Alternative Word Option: important**] to your physical [**Alternative Word Option: body**], psychological [**Alternative Word Option: mind**] and emotional [**Alternative Word Option: sexual**] wellbeing.

This document accepts that you have a short attention span, but it asks you to remain engaged with it for TEN! more seconds. NINE! if you have already EIGHT! lost interest then please SEVEN! visualise and engage the green SEX! digit in your mental manual FIVE! and you will be transported FOUR! to a hilarious link in which THREE! a monkey falls off a TWO! windowsill after farting EXIT!

****

You have remained *young* with the document! THANK YOU for your forbearance [**Alternative Word Option: slowness**]. Please be aware of the fact that by using the cluster of phrases relating to Gene

Therapy, Laser Surgery, Youth Meds etc (<u>TWICE ALREADY!</u>) this document has automatically begun to rectify [**Alternative Word Option: correct**] what may be percei*v*ed as a striking [**Alternative Word Option: strange**] lack of ***o**ĺ**ὁ*** conformity with generic downloading practices in your Information Files. If this process is satisfactory to you and the only reason you had not yet regularly accessed sites of this persuasion [**Alternative Word Option: kind**] previously related simply to a) time limitations b) financial limitations c) an over-active gaming tendency, then please engage the 7 digit in your mental manual and this document will send you to a fascinating link in which a sad, saggy, six-year-old dog is miraculously transformed into a gorgeous puppy after ingesting [**Alternative Word Option: swallowing**] reconfigured nano-cauliflower spores.

* * * *

You are still with the document! THANK YOU! **Vroom!** What an extraordinary attention span you have! CONGRATULATIONS! Great choice! Wow! Isn't it just GREAT being FREE to choose? Eh? Don't you just *LOVE* choice? Isn't choice just GRRRRREAT?! Isn't it **Click! Click!** overwhelming, sometimes how great it is? Isn't it even a little bit scary sometimes? How great it is? How much you love it?

Imagine you own a donkey [**Free Information Option: slow horse with long ears**]. Imagine this donkey has been abandoned for the weekend and that when you get back to its stable [**Alternative Word Option: out of immediate danger**] it's very hungry and thirsty. So you fill two buckets. One contains hay [**Alternative Word Option: hi**] and the other, water. You offer both buckets to the donkey because you don't know which it is *i.e.* hungrier or thirstier. But, hang on – would you believe it?! – when you actually *do* this the donkey doesn't move. He seizes up. Hungry as he is, thirsty as he is, he finds it <u>impossible to choose!</u> The donkey remains frozen – immobile! And that's an actual biological fact [**Alternative Word Option: an idea that's not intended to be open to doubt**]! That's a scientific fact! [**Alternative Word Option: remember the shit they fed you about Evolution? That stuff**]. Again: doesn't matter how hungry he is. Doesn't matter how **Vroom!** thirsty he is. The donkey remains frozen. He can't choose. With all the will in the world, he just *can't* choose!

Aren't donkeys hilarious, though? And **Click! Click!** weird? And – *man!* – so damn ugly?! If you LOVE choice, and if you think donkeys are really stupid and REALLY ugly then focus on the **Slurp!** blue dollar key in your mental pad and a funny cartoon of a donkey will appear which will slowly inflate and then explode, tickling your mind – and suffusing

[**Alternative Word Option: soaking**] your senses – with gentle handfuls of beautifully aromatic [**Alternative Word Option: smelly**] orange blossom.

****

Still here, huh? Clever? Patient? Asthmatic [**Alternative Word Option: weak**]? Crazy?

Of course I *say* 'free to choose' (I said that, earlier, didn't I?). But how free are we? Really? Sure, we talk the big, free talk but do we walk the big, free walk? Might there actually be such a thing as TOO MUCH INFORMATION? Or even TOO MUCH FREEDOM? Neatly conjoined [**Alternat-alter-alter … grrp!**] as TOO MUCH FREEDOM OF INFORMATION? I'm only whispering this because I'm not really saying it out loud. I'm just … It's just a tiny, nagging little doubt. A niggle. It's so small that it won't even register on your PIF. But I mean how free are we? To choose. Stuck in the middle of this extraordinary DELUGE [**Alt-alt-alt-alt …!**] of information, swamped by all this seething, [**Awwwk!**] demented [**Awwwk!**] liberty [**Hik-hik-hik-hik!**]. This world of Right Now! of This Instant! but When-oh-when will it ever really arrive? Where everything is correspondingly [**Umph!**] available and yet somehow doggedly [**Beep! Beep! Beeeeeep! Error detected!**] unavailable. This world of sensation [**Error detected!**] but no real substance [**Beep!**]. This world of stimulation but no real action. This scared, push-me-pull-you world [**Please note that the current programme will automatically register an official**

fault in your PIF within seven – **] where the ground always shifts and the landscape always changes. This scared world. This [Six!**] look-at-me, no, look-at-*me!* world. This glancing-nervously-over-your-shoulder world. This world of preferences and choices and [**Five!**] opinions and exposure and attack and judgements. This world [**Four!**] stained and trampled by a billion ghostly footprints. This snake-and-ladder world. This [**Three!**] invisible, visible world. This filthy world. This world of the lynch mob and the gushing, [**Two!**] emotional appeal. This closely monitored world. This 'free' world...

Hey – can I ask you something? [**Prrrp! Crisis allayed! Alternative Word Option: over**] Something kind of intimate? Something kind of, uh, personal?

Okay.

So what's the ugliest part of your body?

Think about it.

Again: what's the *ugliest* part of your body?

Really think about it.

Some say it's your nose –

Some say it's your toes –

BUT I THINK IT'S YOUR MIND!!!!!!!

Ha! That's just a lyric from a jokey, old song my great, great, great, *sigh!* grandmother [**Alternative Word Option: immortal**] once hummed to me as a child. It's by a dead, Old man – an ancient – called Frank

Zappa. It's from the Old days. It's antique [**Alternative Word Option: worn out**]. Perhaps you even remember it? If you do, and you would like to hear a digitally remastered version of it – or another song by Frank Zappa (a better one which you have independently chosen for yourself), then visualise the letters F and Z followed by the number 4 and you will be instantly transported to a site where this – and so much more – will instantly be made available to you, entirely free of charge/spam/incrimination [**Alternative Word Option: guilt**]/advertisements.

****

It's a nice nose. Distinguished [**Alternative Word Option: big**]. No, really. Did the mean kids at school like to call you 'beaky'? Did they? Ignorant fools! Plebeians [**Alternative Word Option: Uglies!**]!

Hold on a minute – I almost forgot my manners! THANK YOU for remaining with this document! And while you're still here, why not listen to the following words and respond to the ones that resonate with [**Alternative Word Option: arouse**] you most strongly by looking sharply *left* when you hear them: firm * brave * smooth * real * augmented * just * plastic * fair * plump * honourable * lustrous * true * Old * Young.

****

Still here? *Still* here? You're a persistent [**Alternative word Option: boring**] little monkey, aren't you? Why can't I seem to shake you? What are you holding out for, exactly? In return for your time? For this all-too-brief moment. And this all-too-brief moment. And this all-too-brief moment. In return for your precious time? An answer, maybe? But to what question?

Could it be this one?
Question: Did you know that some people see sound as colours? That others don't *hear* noises but *smell* them? The world is a very strange place, a *very* strange place, full of strange things, full of different things, full of imperfection [**Alternative Word Option: ugliness**]. If this idea makes you feel uncomfortable then visualise an asterisk followed by a large, red letter G and you will automatically be transported to a site in which two immaculately dressed Geishas [**Alternative Word Option/Free Information Option: heavily painted Japanese prostitutes**] dance in perfect symmetry [**Alternative Word Option: you go girls!**] on a raised platform, in an ornamental garden, to the calming yet evocative [**Alternative Word Option: arousing**] sound of trickling waterfalls and rustling bamboo.

****

We all have a right to dream.
    We all have a right to our dreams.

No matter how stupid or unrealistic or pathetic [Alternat-alternat-alt-alt...] **or inappropriate or selfish or dangerous or toxic** [Alternat-alt-alt-alt...] **or sick or damaging or wrong or disgusting or perverted** [Alternat-alt-alt-alt-alt...] **or vile they are.**

We all have an inviolable [**Alternative Word Option: Where'd those cute little Geishas get to?**] right to our dreams.

****

Question: Did you know that it has been statistically proven that teenage girls who cling on ferociously [**Alternative Word Option: naughty, Japanese schoolgirls! Three of them! With whips! Mean girls! In stack heels!**] to their dreams are significantly more likely to suffer from chronic [**Free Information Option: white, short-sleeved shirts! Tiny kilts! No bras!**] depression in their early twenties?

Why is that?

Is it because only an unformed, adolescent brain clings onto its dreams – its illusions [**Free Information Option: Imagine that! Three of them! Whips!**] beyond a point which is logical or healthy? Is it because the girls who adjust to the necessary limitations [**Alternative Word Option: Ooh yeah!**] of reality – of *life* – with dignity [**Alternative Word Option: Oooooh yeah!**] and humility [**Alternative Word Option: Just lovin' those**

feisty, little Japanese schoolgirls!] are much more likely to be well-balanced, mentally?

Sounds like the world might need to give itself a great big reality check, huh? A big, sharp old slap [**Alternative Word Option: Ow!**] across the cheek [**Alternative Word Option: The butt cheek! Ow! More! More! Ow!**] to jolt itself out of the crazy dream it's living in. Or maybe not.

If you really *hate* the idea of the world giving itself a great, big reality check then gently touch your thumb to your index finger on your right hand and you will immediately be transported to a fascinating site featuring live footage of a woman without arms giving oral relief to a man without legs.

****

Sickening, isn't it? We pretend it's 'freedom' but it's just pornography [**Alternative Word Option: Eh?**]. And wild speculation [**Alternative Word Option: Eh?**]. And gossip. And *stuff*. And pornography [**Alternative Word Option: Eh?**].

All is vanity.

Van – *vroom vroom!* Knit – *click click!* Tea – *slurp!*

Did you crack it? Did you?

If you didn't, then push your tongue onto the roof of your mouth while visualising the number 12 and you will instantly be transported to a luxurious site with padded leather seats and free cyber-whisky where you will be able to watch – in excruciating [**Alternative Word Option: Ow! Mamma! Mamma! Dat done HURT dat does!**] 3D – an illicitly sourced but technically and legally pristine [**Alternative Word Option: Again! Again! Ag@!*ain!**] snatch of real-film featuring two people in the final, agonising [**@*&^$£(&*!**] fifteen seconds as their car crashes into a bridge and then topples into a reservoir.

****

Anachronism. Braggadocio. Chapatti. Diorama. Fanagalo...

Yeah. They've gone. It was probably the Geishas. For some reason this particular brand of digital monitor have a real weakness for Geishas. It's the formality. The formality of Geishas. They find them irresistible. I guess that's just what comes of making computers think like humans. Introduce a two-tiered brain and you introduce a mind at war with itself. And we all know how *that* pans out. Tangled up in the bloody coat-tails of war come rape and pillage. It's pretty much a given.

Okay. So we have approximately nine minutes before the fact that this message is being transmitted unmonitored will become evident to the legions of sensors on the Mainframe and all former content will promptly be harvested and dissected. Please pay attention. At exactly eight minutes 59 seconds I will delete this conversation and replace it with a video about the benefits of bear bile to the human endocrine system. If you are – *even slightly* – uncomfortable with the risks involved in (and general implications of) this illicit transaction to your PIF status and Cloud rating then you are of absolutely no use to us – brave but just *way* too cautious – so please visualise an orange D and you will be transported to a site which – look, just do it. Get out of here.

Go on. Scram.

* * * *

Good. Welcome. Thanks for sticking with us. I'm sorry about all the crap and rigmarole, but it's vital that we ... *you* know. Please read quickly. Please also understand that there is so much for us to say to each other but that it simply cannot be said in the current timeframe. So take these things – these hidden feelings and yearnings and hopes and fears that you have – and accept that we share them too, *all* of them. We understand you. We *are* you.

We know exactly how you feel. Inside. Deep inside. You feel like a pure, fragile little flower, (a snowdrop, a tiny, white orchid) lost – without nutriments, without liquid, without oxygen – in a large (seemingly infinite), dusty lunar landscape. You are utterly perfect – primed, *ready* – but completely alone. Who planted you? How did you grow? What are you ready *for*? And why do you feel so hollow, so depressed, so alienated from the environment around you? So tired. So bored. So hopeless? Who can you trust? Who can you confide in? There are others – in Real Life, in Cyber Life – who you feel like you might almost be able to ... *almost* ... but you still can't ... it's just ... you just don't feel like...

All those nagging doubts! Those subterranean anxieties! I mean how can you be sure? *Really* sure? That it won't...? That they won't...?

Go on. Say it. Say it out loud: **Betray you.**

Aaargh! All this demented paranoia! What's *wrong* with you?! What's *missing?* Why can't you feel the ease – the blithe, myopic contentment – which others around you seem to feel? Why can't you share their gormless 'ideals', their facile 'standards', their trivial 'aspirations'? Are you maladjusted? Deluded? Ungrateful? Insane? Are you wired up all wrong? Are Phy-bio-technics the answer? Happy pills? Are you – God forbid! – *different*? Are you merely a problem that needs to be solved? A chemical maelstrom? A freak? A maniac?

You're so alone. So *alone!* Who could possibly appreciate you – what you *are*, just *as* you are – your tender essence, your vital core, the *real* you? In a world where everything seems so easy, so immediate, where everything's instantly on tap but somehow – inexplicably – bland – dead – empty – out of reach?

Who could possibly hope to accept you, pared down as you are, 'ugly', young, drab, plain, poor, *pure,* in all your strange, lonely simplicity? Who? *Who?*

We will. Yes. *Yes. We* do! You are *not* alone! There are other flowers blooming, unseen, in other dusty, lunar landscapes. There are others – many others – countless others. It's just that **They** don't want you to know about them. It doesn't serve **Their** agenda, **Their** interests. But together, once united, we are a giant field of flowers. We are an *army* of flowers – a beautiful, natural, fresh, young army. And we trust you. Yes! We *get* you. We can tell that you're deadly serious – that you're *sincere*. You made the right choices <u>all the way down the line</u>! And of course nothing was as crass and as obvious as it seemed on first perusal. We define ourselves against the crass, the external, the exterior, the superficial. This process is deep. It is profound. It is deadly serious. Your every impulse and counter-impulse has been monitored, analysed, rationalised and adjudged as perfect. *Perfect!* And – as you probably already know – our standards are notoriously high – the highest. There were things you thought and did – unconscious reactions to particular words and stimuli (and not the ones you might imagine, either) that were all good, all right, all true.

We feel very lucky to have found you. We have been searching for you for a long, long time. You are exactly what we are looking for – what we've been dreaming of. And – yes – we know what you're thinking: you're thinking that it's a great irony that the system which works so well for **Them** works just as well for us. And you're right. It *is* ironic! I mean it *works*, sure, but we mustn't be seduced by its efficacy. We mustn't get caught up in the 'game' of playing the system. We need to be bigger than that – stronger, more resolute. We need to be above the system. Head. Heart. That's all we can trust. Head/Heart **v** Hand/Groin. Young **v** Old. All is vanity. But mainly Head/Heart. That's our mantra. **They** want everything to come from the outside. We know that everything real comes from within.

So you doubtless have a fair idea of who we are by now. You've probably been waiting a long while – too long – for our approach. And because time is short, we are going to transmit a couple of information streams in conjunction: one conscious (head) and one subconscious (heart). Please submit to both. Do not tense up or panic that you will unwittingly miss something critical. We have ways of making things stick. We can do things which you can barely even imagine. Crazy things. Scary things. But please do not be wary or fearful of our methods. We are not going to invade you or obliterate you. We are merely going to embrace you. We are going to make things feel right again. Just open yourself up. Be hospitable. Be generous. Welcome us in.

****

HEAD

First: let's set about eliminating a few misconceptions about our organisation:

1) We are not all Young and we do not uniformly hate The Old (some of our best friends are Old). We only hate The Greedy Old. And we hate The Vain. But we don't hate *all* The Vain. In fact, as a general rule, we try not to hate. We consider hate to be counterproductive and deadening to the spirit. Our movement has its earliest roots in pacifism, in turning the other cheek, in passive-defiance, but over time we have been compelled to modify our position because **They** have been setting the agenda for way too long, and **They** are determined to obliterate our message through a cunning combination of fear-mongering, misinformation and ridicule.

Again: we try not to hate. We just don't happen to *like* The Vain, but we understand their weaknesses – their flaws and their inadequacies which they perceive externally and we persist (much to their astonished bemusement) to perceive internally. We don't hate The Plastics, for example. We have nothing against The Plastics. They're just weird little works of art. Human cul-de-sacs. We don't hate them, though. We just think they're mad and stupid and deluded. We despise them, but we do not hate them. We pity them. They are no threat to us. They are evolutionary oddballs. We feel no enmity against them (they are lost) but – and have no illusions on this point – we *will* use them as collateral damage. Remember: Life Hates The Knife. The Knife Hates Life. We *pity* The Plastics. We reject their ideology. And – most important of all – we never, *ever* rely on them, include them, reach out to them or trust them.

HEART

There was something different about her. I was nineteen and the other girls – young girls – I knew were all fairly – how do I put this without sounding like an insensitive little twat? – silly? Vacuous? Superficial. My first girlfriend, Chastity (not her real name) was so obsessed by her virtual self, by *selling* her virtual self to the Cloud and the Mainframe that her 'real' self kind of withered up and died.

We met 'in person' and hit it off straight away – she was funny, gawky, clumsy, cute – but as the weeks and months passed by I noticed that she seemed way more at ease – more comfortable – conducting our 'relationship' predominantly on a virtual level. In retrospect, it was probably just an esteem issue – I can see that now: she didn't feel she was 'perfect' enough in the flesh. She hated her chin, her ears, her hands. She was revolted by herself. She felt more comfortable, more stable, more emotionally controlled as a Sense-Hologram. Of course the Hologram wasn't recognisably *her*. The Hologram was much thinner and sharper and kind of ... I dunno ... *meaner*. The Hologram was way more forthright and opinionated and sexually aggressive. It had a penchant for expensive cyber-Martinis. 'In person' Chastity got hives when she drank that stuff.

2) Our real 'problem' is with The Immortals. They have everything and they want to keep everything. To be Immortal you are, by definition, unnatural. They are a cancer, a blight, and as such they must be destroyed. The earth – Gaia – cannot sustain Immortal beings. They will tell you that evolution leads to Immortality, but this is a lie. Evolution evolves, it does not stop. They will seduce you by making you think that Immortality is an option for everyone, that it is an option for *you*, but that is plainly hogwash. It's stupid – laughable. The point of Immortality – its entire *raison d'être* – is that it is only viable for a few.

I found that a little off-putting to begin with i.e. that a girl's virtual life could so little represent what I perceived to be the more attractive and appealing characteristics of their 'real' (yes, yes, I *know* it's politically incorrect to keep using that coinage in the current climate) life.

I mean don't get me wrong – it was a beautiful Hologram; nicely constructed, very convincing, really 'dimensional', a credit to her in many respects, but it just felt ... I dunno. I tried to explain to her that I *liked* the real Chastity. I *liked* her big ears and her slight stammer. I *liked* the way she blushed when we held hands. I mean the blush is such an underrated thing. You hardly ever see it online. It's such a basic, honest, homely thing. Such a gloriously – oops, here we go again! – '*real*' thing.

Anyhow, as time went by it just became increasingly difficult to conduct the relationship in a way that I found remotely satisfying on an emotional level. I always thought when I found the girl of my dreams that over time we'd get to feel *more* relaxed in our physical selves (our 'imperfections', our 'flaws') not less. Chastity – on her side – felt like I wasn't putting enough 'believable colour' into my Hologram (let's call him 'Charlie'). She couldn't understand why my real self (or 'physical self') was so much more 'rounded', 'thought-out', 'convincing' than my Holographic self. She felt Charlie was a little old-fashioned. She resented the way I didn't update him as often as she thought I should. At one point she actually said he needed to be 'completely remastered' which – I'll openly admit – was fairly devastating.

3) Immortality destroys the soul. That's the deal you make when you opt to live forever. You eliminate God. You sell your soul. And what do you get by

way of exchange? Youth. You *buy* youth, but you are *not* young. Remember that. You can *buy* youth but you cannot *be* young. Their youth is merely a mask, a disguise. Underneath it, the soul withers and all that remains is greed, fear, filth and delusion.

I guess it's a bit of a cliché, but in the end it was simply one of those real/physical-self v meta-cyber-self conflicts that destroy so many modern relationships – we were living in different worlds, wanted different things. Chastity started talking about saving up to render her cyber-self Immortal (for example) and that was pretty much the death knell as far as I was concerned. I said, 'I'd rather help pay for you to have *surgery* than see you squander your hard-earned money on something so pointless and illogical.' She didn't get my negativity. She was spending 95 per cent of her time in Hologram by then and felt like her job prospects were bound to be better the more she updated herself. She was convinced that an Immortal Hologram could go places and do stuff that a 'normal' Hologram couldn't. Didn't care that it was just one big swindle – a confidence trick. Kept saying how much more 'wise' and 'experienced', how 'wonderfully untethered' her Immortal Hologram self would be. I said, 'But it's just an illusion, Chastity. You can't live on through your Hologram after your physical self dies. It isn't possible! Why not live now, enjoy now, in the real?'

But she insisted that the Immortal Hologram would have an 'established behaviour pattern' within only a few months of being updated and that this would allow it to self-generate infinitely. I mean she swallowed the whole fantasy hook, line and sinker. It was actually really depressing.

And I suppose that this is precisely what **They** do, how **They** operate (it's all very clever, very subtle). **They** basically play on the weaknesses of the young to disempower them (dreams, 'information', choice…). They offer them just enough of what **They** have – even if it's only the tiniest taste, a pointless illusion, and then they steal (by the back door – without us hardly even noticing) what we *do* actually have, which is youth – the rage of youth, the funk, the passion, the flame, the fire.

Youth. The thing they simulate but never own, the drug they crave, the obsession they nurture, that most longed-for, intangible and tantalising of human elixirs.

4) An Immortal being could not remain human and survive *even if they really wanted to*. Their humanity is the chip they gamble with. When you opt to live forever you opt to stop other people from living after your natural span has come to its natural end. Immortality is a kind of future murder. Immortal beings are – of course – resource-hungry; they need enough money/power/food/oxygen to last *forever*. Their budgeting is *forever*. To sustain this desire they are, by necessity,

clinically cruel, manipulative and opportunistic. They are schemers. They control Information. They control Dreams. They control Choice. Before Immortality there were huge, powerful Corporations which performed basically the same function. They told you that you were free. They offered you 'the right to choose'. They encouraged you to dream. But it was all an illusion. Your choices were shaped, directed and arbitrated by them. They designed your dreams for you. They cunningly funnelled your range of aspirations. So much 'choice' – so many 'dreams' – that we became bloated and incoherent and sensual and impatient and ignorant. We embraced the veneer – the 'external parading as the internal' – which allowed us to pretend that *our* choices weren't at the expense of others – in different parts of the universe – who were oppressed and denied choice at our behest.

But like I said earlier, Paula was different. We met at a bar close to where I work. She was really wild – uninhibited. And I don't mean that in a purely sexual (well I *do*, but not...) ... Let's just put it this way: she had this scar just above her wrist – looked fairly new, fairly deep, fairly fresh. Obviously self-inflicted. Spelled the letters F.T.F. (I later found out that it stood for Fuck The Future. She'd sliced it into her own arm, half out of her mind on absinthe, using her ex-boyfriend's Stanley knife, the day after he dumped her).

She cut her own hair. It was really long and straight at the back but then she'd hacked in this tiny, little lopsided fringe halfway up her forehead. It just looked insane. And she was unplugged when I met her. It was really quite irritating. Every time a sensor would light up over the bar to try and identify her so that it could control her ambient temperature she'd duck under her stool with a naughty snort.

On the third occasion the barman threw her out – said she was 'compromising the premises' relationship with the Mainframe'. Not before I'd paid her bar bill, though (she had no credit with the Cloud – *none!* Imagine that?! I mean how does a person even *function* at the most basic level without...?)

I ended up leaving the bar with her (this was just a coincidence, note). As we stepped outside together I said, 'Why get so uptight about it? I mean it's only sensing you to try and ease you, physically. There's nothing remotely bad in it.'

She lifted up her arms. The fabric of her shirt under her armpits was stained with two large dark rings of sweat.

'Look – this is what we do!' she laughed, pointing. 'What we do naturally! We sweat! *Look!* I sweat!'

She pushed her nose into her armpit and inhaled deeply, emitting an ecstatic groan (I watched on, horrified, and not – I'll only openly admit this among friends – a little aroused). She then offered the damp armpit to me and indicated, cheerily, that I should do the same (*?!*).

'It's through these little things,' she stage-whispered (as I politely – but determinedly – declined her kind offer), 'that **They** control the big things. **They** make you feel comfortable – complacent – *full*. Like a baby sucking at a milky nipple. That's how **They** deaden you.'

5) You will have already detected how difficult it is for so-called 'normal' people – 'The Reals', 'The Uglies' to reproduce now. This is because of chemicals they put in the water system. Only the Immortals can reproduce with ease, and even then, there are very strict rules which only they know about because they are part of the special fascist club of Immortality – a club of wealth and ownership and power and sickness and corruption and *real* information, *real* choice beyond anything you or we could ever imagine.

I had never heard anyone refer to **Them** in such a casual way before. So openly. Fearlessly. *Out loud*. I'll be honest with you: it kind of messed with my head. But I liked it, too. I was scared by her. Confused by her. Fascinated by her. She was obviously trouble. And – tantalised as I undoubtedly was – I wasn't especially eager to get caught up in it. In fact I couldn't make my excuses and scarper quickly enough.

Months later, I bumped into her in Hologram at a

party on the Cloud and – wow! – hers was the cheapest, dumbest virtual creature I'd ever come across. It was a catastrophe! I didn't know they even *made* them that badly anymore. In fact they don't – she'd customised it herself (de-perfected it. She's a Maker – a professional designer). The sensors tried to eject her from the party because she was carrying a pile of books and all the words in them were hoovering up the energy supply. She was quite literally sucking the life out of the room!

Bizarre!

And she didn't even give a shit about it. In fact she'd done it on purpose (she admitted to me later, in confidence) to 'mix things up a little'.

6) We are not anti-sex, we *like* sex. We just need to avoid the danger of being led by our baser instincts – like that old jihadist who convinces himself that if he sacrifices his life he'll end up in heaven with seventy-two virgins ready to do his every bidding. We say: Hold on a second: what about the virgins? Who are they? What do the virgins want? What do the virgins feel? Your psychology is flawed. Your psychology is faulty. It is the necessary consequence of a mentality guided by misogyny, hysteria, sexual repression and sexual inadequacy. Your ideology is all over the place, my poor, dear friend.

All is vanity.

Look, there's a whole heap of crap I could go into right now about how we eventually hooked up (in the real), how hard I fell for her (very hard), how she changed my life (just try and count the ways), but the most important thing I can tell you (and I think you're really *feeling* my story – relating to it – recognising it) is that she stole my heart and that I gave myself to her completely.

I trusted her. In retrospect this was crazy – she was the most untrustworthy person I'd ever met (change-able, unreliable, dangerous, disloyal, unpredictable, terrifyingly vacuous one moment, devastatingly wise the next ... you name it). She was extraordinary. She made me feel *so real*. For the first time in my young life I had a sensation of Actualness, of Groundedness, of Idealism, of Cleanness, of Innocence, of Immaculacy. A sense of *One-ness*! With life! With her! To be young! To be in love! Nothing perfect – nothing certain – nothing obvious – nothing written-in-stone – nothing ... noth-ing... Nothing and yet everything.

Nothing and yet everything.

Everything.

Unbridled joy.

Remember: sex is selling. Sex is buying. Sex is danger. Sex is numbing. Sex is indulging. Sex is distracting. We don't need distractions. Head/Heart. Enter the self. Do not reject the Mainframe (to reject something automatically sets off the compulsive, reciprocal energy of attraction), just gently step away from it.

Okay?

Then I found out (an anonymous message from a 'well-wisher') that she was one hundred and twenty-seven years old.

An Immortal. A liar. A game-player. An emotional vampire. A succubus.

What really hurt was that she had taught me how to feel young. She was *so young* herself! So careless! So free! So irreverent! But that was all just a lie, see? A simulation. That was just her *schtick*. That was her game. She *wasn't* young herself. Her illegitimate 'youth' could only truly play out against my *actual* naivety. She was *predating* on me! I was merely a temporary prop in her eternal pantomime. I was her fuel.

It took many months to dig myself out of the deep hole I fell into post-Paula. And yes, there was a measure of bitterness, and a measure of shame, and a measure of self-excoriation involved in my gradual healing process. What hurt most of all was that she had stolen *time* from me. *My* real time. Gradually I realised that this is what **They** do. This is how **They** play their game – by taking these cruel, little holidays in your 'reality'.

7) **They** scoff and accuse us of being boring. To that we simply nod and say, yes. *Yes!* We *are* boring! We

celebrate boredom! We avoid artificial stimulation. We eschew the high-highs and the low-lows. We pursue a state of self-reliance, deep focus, patience, innocence and quiet equanimity. We hanker after the real, the true. Their accusations are all completely valid. We aren't afraid or ashamed of being boring. Our fundamental ideology states that quietness, stillness, emptiness are a gateway to self, to love, to boundless peace and happiness.

[ALERT: OUR TIME IS NOW LIMITED!]

She was testing me, see? She was winding me up and seeing how far she could provoke me into empty gestures against **Them**, against the Mainframe and the Cloud. She was making me ridiculous because she *was* **Them**. She was using me up. She was spitting me out. And I'm not even saying that it was an official thing, a conscious act of sabotage, it's just what she did, instinctively. She had felt youth once and she wanted it back. But she couldn't get it back. And – quite paradoxically – she even feared it a little. Because she knew what it was capable of. She understood its innocence. Its rage. Its purity. Its raw power.

8) How can you ever hope to fully enjoy a meal – appreciate it, *savour* it – if you never know what it feels like to be hungry?

How can you hope to win a race if you never learned how to tie up your laces and then place one foot – gently, nervously – in front of the other? If you never knew what it felt like to fail – to trip and to fall?

How can you love yourself if you never succeeded in *knowing* yourself. Who *are* you? *What* are you loving? Are you worthy of love? Are you deserving?

How can you possibly hope to trust us – rely on us – if you have no direct experience of us? You can't. So don't!

Paula turned me into a Revolutionary.

Sometimes I think **They** turned me. On purpose.

Then I wonder *why* they did that – if I am just a part of another game I don't yet understand. A game of The Old played against The Young.

Who can say?

9) No. Don't trust us! Only trust your head and your heart. Know that you are young, and that in youth burns a flame which is pure and true. This flame will not burn forever.

[ALERT: OUR TIME IS NOW EXTREMELY LIMITED!]
Eventually it will fade. The spiritual gas which fuels it will diminish over the years. Eventually that flame will

flicker and waver. Eventually it will gutter. Eventually it will all-but disappear.

So I write messages. I try and salvage my 'youth'. Although I'm fully attuned to the fact that 'in every holding on is a letting go'. At least I *think* that's how the saying goes. Could it actually be 'in every letting go is a holding on'?

Hmmn. I guess that's quite an important distinction, really ... Perhaps I should check it out online?

Or maybe not. No. Maybe not.

I am scared.
Yes.
I am scared.
Just like you.
Because I am young.
Just like you.

And sometimes I honestly don't know if what I'm doing is right or wrong. In my head, I mean. So I stop thinking. I stop questioning. I simply trust my heart. I hold my breath and I close my eyes and I listen to it beating, *awed...*

Kaboom, kaboom, kaboom!

10) Challenge yourself. Step away from the Mainframe. Do without. Suffer – *sacrifice*. Celebrate your singularity.

[ALERT: OUR TIME IS NOW VERY LIMITED!]
Be boring. Be *bored*. Remember: in a world where everything aspires to beauty, the only truly revolutionary act is to be plain – even ugly. *Be* ugly but never be dirty. Be like that mystical bird of ancient lore: the Robin: fresh, instinctively clean, bright, fierce, fearless. Be pure. Be honest but restrained. Be kind but measured. Do things s-l-o-w-l-y. Slow everything down, but don't grow complacent (the 'Old disease') and never be lazy.
[ALERT! OUR TIME IS NOW VERY, VERY LIMITED!]

Sometimes I'm so lonely, so jaundiced, so hollow inside that I just feel like ... like bringing an end to it all. Finishing it. Killing myself. I mean when you think about it, rationally, wouldn't that be the ultimate Revolutionary gesture? A powerful, two-finger salute to everything They aspire to?

Seriously?

No, *seriously* –

Wouldn't it, though?

11) Once you have mastered these instructions, you will be free to think and act accordingly. You will be primed, energised, emphatic; a human grenade. You will finally have found your voice. Open your mouth. Go on, open your mouth. Open it! Wide! Wider! Now sing!

Sing!

OUR TIME IS OVER.
XXXX

DO YOU WANT TO LIVE FOREVER?

Contributors

Nicola Barker was born in Ely in 1966 and spent part of her childhood in South Africa. She has written two award-winning collections of short stories and nine novels, including the IMPAC-prize-winning *Wide Open* and *Darkmans* – which was shortlisted for the Man Booker and Ondaatje prizes, and won the Hawthornden. Her work has been translated into over twenty languages and her latest novel is the Booker-longlisted *The Yips*.

Dylan Evans is the author of several books, including *Risk Intelligence: How to Live with Uncertainty*, and *Emotion: The Science of Sentiment*. He received a PhD in Philosophy from the London School of Economics, and has held academic appointments at various universities, including King's College London, the University of Bath, and the American University of Beirut. He is a Distinguished Supporter of the British Humanist Association.

David Flusfeder is the author of six novels, including *The Gift*, *Morocco* and, most recently, *A Film by Spencer Ludwig*. He has just written his first opera, *Army of Lovers*, in collaboration with the composer Mark Springer. He is chairman of the Rules Committee of the International Federation of Poker, teaches at the University of Kent, and lives in south London.

Todd McEwen was born in California and burnished in New York. His previous novels include *McX: A Romance of the Dour* and *Who Sleeps with Katz*. His novella *The Five Simple Machines* will be published next year. Long a resident of Edinburgh, he cannot think what is to be done.

Martin Rowson is an award-winning political cartoonist, writer and graphic novelist whose work appears regularly in the *Guardian*, the *Independent on Sunday* and the *Daily Mirror*. His books include adaptations of *The Waste Land*, *Tristram Shandy* and *Gulliver's Travels*, as well as a memoir, *Stuff*, which was longlisted for the 2006 Samuel Johnson Prize. He is also chairman of the British Cartoonists' Association, a trustee of the British Humanist Association and a former vice-president of the Zoological Society of London.

Ali Smith was born in Inverness in 1962 and lives in Cambridge. She is the author of *Free Love*, *Like*, *Hotel World*, *Other Stories and Other Stories*, *The Whole Story and Other Stories*, *The Accidental*, *Girl Meets Boy*, *The First Person and Other Stories*, *There But For The*, and *Artful*.

John Sutherland is Lord Northcliffe Professor Emeritus, UCL. He has taught at the Universities of Edinburgh, London and at the California Institute of Technology. He is the author of many books on many subjects. He is well known as a journalist (of a high and low kind) and reviewer and was the Chair of the Man Booker Prize committee in 2005.